RECKONING ON THE GULF

A NOVEL BY

PHILLIP DUNN

PUBLISHED BY FIDELI PUBLISHING, INC.

Cover art by Josh Gregorsok

$1 from every book sold will be donated to

Parkland Foundation Burn Camp.

Camp I-Thonka-Chi is a summer camp for

children that have been burned.

It gives them a chance to be a kid again,

if only for a short while.

I dedicate this book to my wife, Alisa. Without her support, understanding, and opinions I really don't think the work would be what it is. This may sound corny because everybody dedicates a book to their wife but in this instance she was my sounding board, advisor and friend.

We sat in a café on Captiva Island one afternoon. I said to her, "I'm going to do something very different."

The idea was only a seed planted in my mind at that time, I had not even hinted to anyone.

She smiled that special smile she possesses and said,

"You're going to write a book."

Acknowledgements

I would like to acknowledge two big influences that got this project going and kept the wind in my sails.

Randy Wayne White, with his Doc Ford series, instilled an overwhelming curiosity in my mind that I had to satisfy. The way he weaves a plot and tells a story made me want to figure out how that is done. His advice was "Just write."

James Waylon Long has the enthusiasm of a great Texas story teller. His advice on writing and publishing kept me going when enthusiasm lagged.

Thank you, gentlemen.

Smoke Showing

"Engine 7 on scene. We have a single story frame structure, smoke and fire showing. Engine 7 will catch the plug on the road and forward lay in. Engine 7 will be attack, next arriving back us up."

"Truck 2 to Engine 7, wrap the plug and go on in. We are right behind you, we will hook you up."

"Engine 7 received. Truck 2 prepare to set a ventilation fan once you get up here."

"Truck 2 received. Vent fan."

Mack told his driver and firefighter, "I know this house; it's Buster Crabtreee's. He's in the hospital and lives alone, so it's probably vacant but we will search as we go. Bear, spot the engine right in front, we are going to pull the number 1 line."

Bear, the driver, said, "Okay, Mack. It looks like all the fire is at the back. Ya'll just push it on out."

"Yeah, Eric, I'll do a 360 of the house while you get the hose set. Wait for me to come back around before you go in. Damn, it's hard to see with all this rain."

Eric, the rookie firefighter, confirmed the order saying, "Got'cha, Loo." (short for Lieutenant).

Bear parked the engine where he was told. He locked the brakes and placed it in pump gear, ready to pump water when the lines were set to go in. He bellowed at Eric, "Come on, rookie, let's go get your gear dirty!"

Mack pulled the straps of his self-contained breathing apparatus tight on his shoulders and jumped off the engine. He took his Maglight, and as Eric was getting the hose in place he circled the house. Twice he tripped on stuff and fell, he thought, *Dammit, Buster, clean this place up!*

He found fire coming from a window and the eaves in one corner of the house. He made a mental note, *Looks like the kitchen or utility room; maybe it's in the attic too. We will have to pull ceiling.* He called Bear on the radio, "Engine 7 officer, Engine 7 driver get me a pike pole to the door."

"Received."

He continued his walk around the house. It was raining so hard he couldn't see much but he saw no fire through the windows; they were just black in the dark. He thought, *If it's not in the attic, we will just walk through this and put it out.* The heavy smoke was hugging the ground. The smoke had an acrid smell to it, odd but nothing to register an alarm with him.

As he rounded the last corner of the house, he saw Eric was like a dog on a chain and ready with the line at the door. The supply line from the plug was swollen with the water pressure from the fire hydrant and the 1-3/4 inch hand line was rigid with the 110 psi Bear was pumping to it. The show was ready to begin.

He got to the front door and grabbed the pike pole. He told Eric, "Kick the door, then I'm gonna pull some ceiling before we go in. I want to make sure we don't have any fire above us."

Eric nodded and kicked the door.

With a swirl of smoke and a brilliant flash of orange Mack's world went black. He saw Tammy Wynette riding a white horse and she was singing "Amazing Grace." Behind her walked a man about three feet tall playing the bagpipes. They were in a rodeo arena and as the bucking chutes opened, goats came out instead of bucking bulls. He felt at peace with this.

Mack was shaken out of this vision by the rain and Bear. He was screaming, "Mack! Mack! Mack!" Mack was holding a helmet against his chest and he couldn't open his hands to drop it. He was confused. He could hear chaos around him.

"Give me a second alarm!"

"Two men down! Send two ambulances!"

"This is now a defensive fire!"

"Get the medical kit!"

"Get those lines over here!"

"Does he have a pulse?"

"Back up!"

"Where is that damn ambulance?"

"Start CPR!"

That statement cleared the fog a little. He turned his head to the side and saw the firefighters crouching over a smoldering pile. He thought, *What is that?* They were tearing the smoldering pile apart to reveal a person. He couldn't believe what he was seeing. The person was a firefighter. Mack began to scream, "Eric! Where is Eric?"

Bear tried to calm him down and said, "We are on it, Mack. Ya'll are hurt. Wait for the ambulance."

"Is that Eric?"

"Yeah, Mack, he's hurt. We are on it."

Mack saw his brother firefighters start chest compressions on his rookie and he felt old black feelings well up in his gut — sorrow, terror, despair.

The ambulances got to the scene. For the badly injured firefighter it was a "throw and go," they put him on the stretcher and quickly put him in the ambulance. The firefighter doing chest compressions climbed on the stretcher with him and never stopped his efforts.

The ambulance had an on scene time of less than a minute. The paramedics intubated him and started two IVs enroute. The medics that came to Mack were met with a combative patient. Mack cussed them and said, "I'm fine, help Eric! Leave me the hell alone. Get over there and help him!"

Roy, the lead medic, said, "Loo, he is already on the way. We are here to help you, brother. You are hurt, let us do our job, man. Let go of that helmet, I need your arm."

"How is he?"

"I don't know; I came straight to you. Ya'll are going to the same hospital. We will find out when we get there. Now calm down and let us work. Okay?"

"Let's get going. Come on! Let's go!"

When he got to the hospital it was pandemonium. Everyone was rushing around from room to room. Nurses were yelling and doctors were trying to be in charge. Injured firefighters got a lot of attention. Mack was evaluated by the ER doc but he was a lesser consideration than the firefighter patient in Trauma Room 1. The doctor wouldn't give him any information on Eric, he only said, "We are doing all we can."

Suddenly all the fast activity stopped. Mack could see the change from his room and he knew what this meant. When a sullen nurse came in to check on Mack he asked, "He's gone, isn't he?"

She was fighting tears while she replied, "We did all we could."

By this time firefighters, both on duty and off duty, had started filtering into the ER. Against the futile arguments of the hospital staff, they started gathering in the Trauma room 1 and Mack's room. The big dirty silent men gathered around their fallen brothers, challenging any intruders. It was like a herd of elephants guarding one of their own.

Get Back on that Horse

Mack sat in his rocking chair on the porch of his ranch house at the Dead Dog Ranch. He had a cup of coffee, a dip of snuff, and a mind full of questions. The cold heaviness of the pre-dawn atmosphere laid on him like a shroud. It seemed to him dawn had always been this way, heavy, darker, and biting just before the sunrise. Then the sun would come up, the burden would evaporate and a bright new day would begin. Life had enveloped him like the heavy air that chilled his bones and he wondered if there would ever be a sunrise in his soul again.

He also was trying to figure out the chain of events that had brought a beautiful woman to his bed. He hadn't been drunk for some time, but it reminded him of past times when he woke up wondering what had happened the night before.

It had all started innocently enough when Samantha Nawaji, the woman in his bed, came into his saddle shop. Sam, as she was called, was the same height as Mack. She could look him straight in the eye when they talked. And she did. Sam had a very direct approach when speaking to someone. Femininity was not her strong suit and she was just the north side of pretty, but she had an air about her that men found confusingly attractive.

Her father was from the Sioux tribe, which could explain her skill with horses. Back in the day, the Sioux were known to be the finest horsemen of the plains. Her mother was German. Sam had long black hair that she mostly kept in a braid. She had the athletic body of a woman that spent all day in the saddle. Her dark eyes could stare a hole in a man.

Sam was a trainer of cutting horses; some said she was a horse whisperer. A horse whisperer has an ability to connect with horses by their mere presence. She could just touch a spooky horse for a while and calm the animal with some sort of unspoken connection.

Sam could do the same thing with Mack. She could extinguish any of his incendiary outbursts with just a word and a look. It confused him as to how she did this, but he liked it.

Sam was also a woman who understood the power of the bosom. Her regular attire was a pearl snap shirt and Wrangler blue jeans but, Mack began to notice, if she needed some leatherwork done she would dress to do business. If it was a small job such as a minor repair, new spur straps or a set of reins, the attire of choice would be a low cut T-shirt. If it was a lot of work to be done, a new pair of chaps or her saddle was broken, she would wear a white tank top without a bra. Mack suspected he was the only man she used this bargaining chip on. Today, a jug-headed horse had torn the fender off of her saddle, possibly breaking the saddle tree. It would be a big job and she knew it. Today she was doing business.

Sam pretty much had no use for men. Except for Mack. She enjoyed his six-foot triangular frame, broad shoulders and a narrow butt. He was well muscled, like a man unafraid of hard work. His skin was tanned from being outside, a place he preferred. She did, too — her office was in the sun. His face was hard from years of seeing so much on emergencies, but his heart was soft also from seeing so much. He had been there when people were having their worst day so he had empathy for the human race. Likewise he could be a very hard and unforgiving man. He was very black and white but could go grey when the situation required it. She admired him for his many facets; she had never known a man so deep. Sam enjoyed his company. He was a quiet man who could speak without talking.

She had her horses and that was all she cared about. This was proven countless times around the stables when the rich cutting horse boys would try a shot at her, only to be unceremoniously put in their place. Many would try; many would fail. Bad horses were her specialty and maybe she saw Mack as a bad horse. Whatever the case, she liked Mack and he liked her. They did not speak of it; they just shared the connection and didn't get in each other's way. They did not date but when either one needed the other they seemed to end up together.

So, as far as he could figure it, she had sensed his despair yesterday and one thing led to another.

As the morning sun came on up to start the day, Mack could hear Sam rummaging around in the kitchen for a coffee cup. Sam liked the way Mack made his coffee but needed a little milk to take the edge off. He brewed it the cowboy way. She came out on the porch to sit with him wearing only an Indian blanket to ward off the morning chill. He admired her sense of style.

With a lilt in her voice Sam said, "G'morning cowboy."

He replied, "G'morning sunshine." Speaking to her and the day too.

After sitting in silence a while and letting the sun come on up, Mack asked, "What do you have going today?"

"Well, I have to work on that blue roan gelding for a while this morning. I think he is ready to put on some calves. Then a man is bringing in another horse for me to put a handle on. What about you?"

Mack said, "I have to be at the fire station in about an hour. How about if I run you by your place on my way to work?"

Sam said, "I hope it goes okay for you, first shift back and all. You going to be okay with it?"

"Yeah. At least I'll be back with my crew. We can start working through it. Just gotta get back on the horse that threw you, as they say."

Mack didn't let on about how he thought his day at work wouldn't be so good. He had been given a shift off to recuperate. In a situation like this, things can happen fast and he hadn't been there to keep up with it. Bear had come by to check on him and told him the rumor was the chief was going to call him downtown when he got back. Nobody knew what for though, it was strictly rumor.

CHAPTER 2

Old Smoke, New Smoke

Mack pulled into the station parking lot right at shift change, he usually didn't cut it so close but he had taken a little extra time in telling Sam goodbye when he dropped her off at the stables. He sat in his truck a few minutes trying to visualize how this day was going to pan out. He wished he had never left the porch.

As he lumbered into the gear room to get his firefighting gear, he noticed he was alone in the apparatus bay — just him, the ambulance and the big red fire engine. He was gratified by this, since he really wanted no interaction today. As he removed the fire coat, bunker pants and helmet belonging to the man that worked yesterday from the fire engine, he could smell fresh smoke on the gear. He thought to himself, *They must have had another fire.*

He placed his gear on the fire engine, smelling his old smoke as he did. He told himself to clean his gear today to make that reminder go away. He checked his self-contained breathing apparatus to make sure he had a full air bottle and arranged his gear so he could dress quickly. He paused, took a deep breath which was cluttered by the old smoke, and apprehensively went into the day room.

Inside the station it was the usual shift change. Men were telling their relief man what had happened the day before, somebody was telling a bad joke, the TV news was on, the grumpy "old heads" were waiting to go home, and the rookies were cooking breakfast. Mack noticed the trash hadn't been emptied and the flags hadn't been put up; today he really didn't care.

When Mack walked in and was noticed, the room fell quiet. The only sound was the newsman on TV and sizzling bacon in the kitchen. When firemen fail to mouth off to each other, there is a problem. Mack noted this and brushed it off as he went to find the Lieutenant he was relieving from duty.

"Hey, Jake. I got ya. Y'all do anything?" Mack asked.

Jake responded, "Aw, we had a little barn fire around midnight, nothing to write home about. How ya doing, brother?" When firemen are social or serious they call each other brother. Jake and Mack had been through a lot together in the 15 years they had worked together. They had fought many fires together and off duty they organized the annual fishing trip. That fishing trip was in its 12th year and was the social event of the season for those that went. Mack had also been on the ambulance run when Jake's father passed away. Mack had done CPR on the man. Jake and Mack were tight.

So, Mack lied as he said, "Aw, I'm fine. Still got a job to do and get along with it."

Jake stared at him a minute, not believing a word of it then said, "If you need anything, don't hesitate."

Mack said, "Thanks, man. I'll get through it, if I can just get through today."

The intercom cracked open, letting everyone know breakfast was on the table. Jake said, "I'll let ya go. Hang tough, brother. Let's go fishing some time."

That thought gave Mack a break in the cloud cover of his grey mood. He certainly did wish he was in the harbor of Port Mansfield watching the sun break into the day. He couldn't remember a bad time on a fishing trip. Even when he and Jake were almost drowned in a sudden storm off shore, it was oddly fun and built a lot of character between the two men.

Thirty men, mostly firemen, went on that trip, and there had never been a major argument or fight. The only rules for coming on the trip were you had to be 21 and a non-asshole. It was simple and seemed to have worked. Life was simple on the trip.

At the breakfast table it was the usual crew, with the exception of one nervous young man newly assigned to the station to replace the man they'd lost. He hadn't yet found his place in the social strata of his new station. A fire crew is like a family, or a pack of dogs, depending on how you looked at it. Either way, you earned your place in line. He was fully aware that this hierarchy had been upset by an on-duty death and it would be a while before all would settle down so he would fit in and be a "bubba."

The young firefighter he was replacing was competent and well liked, and he had attained bubba status very quickly. The fidgety fella knew when he was referred to as a bubba then it would be all right and he would have a place in line.

Mack was the senior man and also the Officer in Charge. His place was leader of the pack. All of the men had a deep respect for him as a firefighter and a man.

The breakfast table was oddly quiet and Mack liked it that way on this day, especially since he wished he was still on the porch with Sam and her blanket. Every once in a while, someone would take a stab at conversation but it died quickly. Really no one knew what to say to lighten the mood.

Firemen usually joke about bad things and laugh them off to decrease impact. Regular people outside the profession find these conversations crude, cold and callous. But firemen are not regular people. Making light of a bad situation is a survival tool they have developed. They take a bad event, and there are many of them, and put it in a box in their mind. They put a lid on that box and do everything in their power to keep the lid on. The box goes on a shelf in their mind. As they go through life and laugh about what is in the box or have serious conversations with brothers about what is in the box, then the box gets smaller. But the lid can never be taken completely off. If the lid ever comes off the box, the problem inside could be crippling and the box could come back bigger than it began. With time the box would eventually get small enough to fall through the slats on the shelf where it could fall into the subconscious mind and be gone, for the most part.

The only people that can help firefighters with sizing their boxes are other firefighters who have boxes themselves. Normal people cannot understand the firefighter psyche — it scares them — so firefighters take care of firefighters. Generally speaking, firefighters will not or cannot have deep conversations about their troubles with people outside the profession. Hence, the brotherhood.

Today, no one was too sure about how to go about packing the box, even Mack. And until the lid was on the box, it couldn't be spoken to. Today was not jokeable, and it might never be. A man had been killed.

Mack usually gave the orders of the day at breakfast, but today he just sat and ate in silence. His silence increased the volume of tension at the table. The tension was broken by the hotline phone ringing and two rookies erupting from the table, racing to be the first to answer it before the second ring. The new guy just sat there with a "what the hell?" look on his face. In the race, one guy body-checked the other right into the coffee table, smashing it to pieces. Mack thought, *Well, that will be a memo,* but it was way down on his list of priorities.

The winning rookie breathlessly got to the phone on the third ring and answered it with, "Station 7, firefighter White speaking." He then said only, "Yes, sir." Firefighter White then solemnly turned and said, "Lt. McWherter, it's the Chief for you."

Mack got up from the table and walked to the phone like he was pulling two tractor tires behind him. He told the rookie to clean up the mess, took the phone and said two things. "Lieutenant McWherter … yes, sir."

He hung up the phone and turned to the audience, "Guys, we have to be at the Chief's office in 30 minutes. Let's get cleaned up."

CHAPTER 3

Bucked Off Again

The ride to the Fire Administration office was quiet. Mack was busy trying to figure out what was going to happen. A call to come downtown wasn't to be taken lightly in the fire service. The other two men, Bear and the new firefighter, were just busy being quiet. It was a pregnant silence.

As Engine 7 was proceeding through Engine 2's district, a dispatch for Engine 2 and Medic 2 came on the radio. It was dispatched as an unknown medical emergency, which could be anything from a heart attack to a hangnail. The address given was the next cross street on engine 7's route. Mack keyed his radio microphone and said, "Engine 7 to dispatch."

Dispatch returned, "Engine 7 go ahead."

Mack said, "Engine 7 is closer to that call; we will jump the run." Mack told his driver to hit the lights and siren and head that way. Dispatch came back on the radio, "Negative engine 7, engine 2 will take the run, per the Chief. Engine 7 is to continue on assignment."

Hearing those instructions tightened Mack's stomach. *This is getting very heavy.* For his attendance at Administration to be required over tending to a medical emergency was ominous.

As Engine 7 pulled into the parking lot of the main Fire Department office, Mack told his guys, "Ya'll just take a radio and hang out in the property room. If we get a run, I will meet you at the engine. And see if you can score me a new cap from Doug." Doug was the Property Master, the dispenser of all Fire Department supplies. He was a good man to be in favor with in the Fire Department. He was also entertaining to talk to, so Mack didn't think his guys would mind being there for a while. He didn't know how long this would take but he was hoping for short and sweet.

Mack trudged up the stairs to the Chief's office with the same enthusiasm as he'd answered the phone at the station. He was met at the top of the stairs by an Assistant Chief, a friend of his, who said "Hey, Mack.

How ya doin'? Have a seat in his office, he will be right in."

Mack could tell his friend was in full-blown Assistant Chief mode and small talk was not the order of the day. He took a seat in the semi-comfortable chair in front of the Chief's desk. He sat there and took in the room around him. There were a myriad of fire service and management books on the bookshelves. Also on the shelves were antique brass fire hose nozzles and fire-related tools. Spaced around the room on the floor were larger nozzles called play pipes and antique copper fire extinguishers. Hanging on the walls were old fire helmets, framed certificates, fire axes, and lots of photographs — photographs of fires, car wrecks, and other catastrophes.

One photograph in particular stood out to Mack. It was a photograph of the Chief as a younger man. He stood in front of a burned out building grinning broadly. Mack could tell by the condition of the building and the dirty haggard faces of the tired men in the background that it had been one hell of a battle. But there stood this young firefighter, grinning as if taking part of the credit for extinguishing this structure fire. He didn't have so much as a smudge of soot on his fire gear, and that bothered Mack.

In walked Fire Chief Alexandro Fuentes, breaking Mack's train of thought. "Big Al" as he was known behind his back was a man of great girth who had oily, slicked back hair. The Chief wore a dress blue uniform, as was his habit. The men were issued one set of dress blues for special occasions and funerals; the Chief had two, his everyday set the same as issued to the men, and another ensemble that would make a Mexican General envious. It was decorated with all sorts of stars, bars, stripes and medals, yet no one knew what they were for. He wore this uniform to all interactions with the public. Showmanship was his forte. Mack remembered that his father referred to people like this as having "all hat and no cattle."

Mack stood as the Chief entered the room. The two men shook hands and the Chief said, "Good morning, Lieutenant." Chief Fuentes then sat down in his overstuffed leather upholstered office chair across the desk from Mack. He stared at Mack a moment then said, "How are you doing, Lieutenant?"

"I'm fine, Chief. How are you?" Mack responded.

The Chief stared a moment longer then cocked his head a little and squinted his eyes, as if to get a better focus. "I mean, how are you *really* doing?"

Mack sensed a verbal chess game coming and he was a man that usually played checkers. His back tensed up and he sat a little straighter in a chair that was becoming more uncomfortable by the second. Because Mack was carrying a great emotional burden from the fire, this conversation in this environment was making him feel worse, so he lied, "I'm doing fine, Chief, considering this past week. The Doc at the ER gave me a clean bill of health. After that one shift of sick leave, I am back feeling okay."

"Yes, Lieutenant, the events of the past week are exactly why we are here today. The Crabtree Ranch fire was a horrible event that injured you and was fatal for firefighter Eric Wilson. It is my understanding that you were friends with Wilson off duty." He wanted to prove to Mack he had done some research.

Still confused as to the direction this meeting was taking, Mack responded, "Yes, sir. We were friends. We hunted and fished together. I think I am part of the reason he hired onto the fire department."

As the Chief stared some more, Mack wondered what his game was and wished he'd quit the staring part. Big Al finally broke the stare, looked at the ceiling and said, "Lieutenant, that is my concern for you."

His gaze drifted from the ceiling back to Mack. "Here you have a rookie firefighter that was also your friend. He was under your command, and due to unfortunate circumstances he is killed and you are injured."

The Chief took a deep breath, stared for effect and at the same time evaluated Mack for any weakness and continued. "This causes me great concern for your emotional well being. I have just returned from a seminar on PTSD in Fort Worth. It dealt with the fire service and the firefighter psyche. The synopsis of the seminar was that old school firefighters, such as yourself, don't talk about their problems and feelings. This practice of not venting fears, frustrations and anxieties leads to other more tangible problems in life and command. It is my duty, as a concerned Fire Chief, to bring the Fire Department into a more modern thought process and secure the emotional well being of my men. Lieutenant, there is a new age dawning in the fire service and we must embrace it."

Mack sat there trying to process what the Chief was saying. He was astonished at Big Al's tirade. *The chief surely isn't gonna try to take that lid off my box. I would never open up to that pompous ass. This man has no idea how real firefighters act or adapt to adversity. The most adverse circumstance he ever faced was a coffee stain on his nice white shirt.*

Chief Fuentes continued to push, "Lieutenant, I would be happy to talk this through with you. I have had extensive training on critical incident debriefing. We also have, through a local church, a chaplain you could talk to. But my professional recommendation would be for you to make an appointment with the psychiatrist the city has on retainer. A professional psychiatrist can help you discover things about yourself that you may not know."

Mack was dumfounded that the Chief, without any previous conversation, background, or knowledge of his history, would recommend that he see a shrink. The only sense he could make of it all was the fire, since there was a firefighter fatality, was high profile and all over the media. Big Al was probably just trying to show the media how compassionate he was toward his men. It had been evidenced to Mack many times that the Chief couldn't care less about the members of the Fire Department. It was all about Fire Chief Alexandro Fuentes, and Mack was not going to buy into it.

So, Mack chose his words carefully when he said, "Chief, I appreciate your concern and your offer. I have been through hard times before and have overcome those problems. It seems to me that old school ways work for old school firemen. I also have to help my crew through this difficult time. We are a family and when the time is right, we will talk it out and get past it, in our own way."

Mack was responding exactly as the Chief had expected. There was no stare this time as he snapped back, "Lieutenant, besides one little class in your continuing education classes at the station, I don't think you have any sort of training relevant to this situation. I don't think you can adequately help yourself, much less your men. I can show you many studies and statistics that will illustrate the negative impact you would have by trying to handle this yourself! As I said before, the new fire service is more sensitive to the needs of firefighters. I would still urge you to use professional assistance."

Mack repeated, "Thank you again, Chief, but firemen know how to help firemen. Always have and always will. We will handle it within the brotherhood and we will be fine."

At the mention of brotherhood, Big Al slammed his fist on the desk and halfway got out of his chair. With a face tight with anger and a piercing stare he bellowed, "This brotherhood you speak of is outdated, there is no brotherhood! All you have is a clique of bubbas and rednecks! The new fire service is a professional and technical job, that's it! A job! Do your job! There will be no cliques in my fire department!"

The marquee lights for the movie he felt like he was living at the moment suddenly came on in Mack's mind. Big Al was never accepted into the brotherhood of firefighters or he had never accepted it. Mack had seen this type of man before, men that got on the fire department to be a chief with no intention of ever learning to be a firefighter. The photograph on the wall explained it, Big Al had never gotten honest dirt on his gear so consequently he'd never been included, nor had he cared to be. His only goal had been to wear that second set of dress blues. There was no way for him to understand Mack's viewpoint because he hadn't lived it. So he had to rely on all of his seminars, studies and statistics to make a good showing. Mack also realized suddenly that he was in a minefield without a map.

Trying to de-escalate the situation, Mack calmly responded, "Chief, to the majority of the members of this fire department the fire service is more than a job — it is a lifestyle, an identity and a family."

Big Al felt that he was losing his composure and tried to calm himself down by shuffling through some papers and not looking at Mack. After a minute he took a deep breath and in a calmer voice asked, "Are you familiar with NFPA 1500?"

Mack was thankful this was one of the few things he remembered from studying for promotional tests. "Yes, sir. That is the National Fire Protection Association standard dealing with firefighter safety and health."

"Very good, Lieutenant. Yes, firefighter health, and included in that is emotional health. Have you ever been to the website www.everyonegoeshome.com?"

"No, sir."

A little calmer now, the Chief continued, "There is a page on that website pertaining to mental health in the modern fire department. I suggest you read it."

"Yes, sir. I will."

"Lieutenant, when you look over NFPA 1500 and visit that website, you will see the modern fire service is now taking a proactive approach to mental health. We have available to us outside assets we will utilize to the advantage of our members. We will modernize our methods. Do you understand what I am saying to you, Lieutenant?"

Mack felt like he was being led into a blind canyon. He understood what the Chief was saying but he was unsure of what unstated message he was trying to convey. With a concerned look on his face Mack responded, "Sir, I agree that we should utilize all available assets and use them in our established methods but what are you saying exactly? I feel like I'm missing something here."

Exasperated and red-faced Chief Fuentes exclaimed, "Lieutenant, you cannot decline my offer of assistance. You must comply with my orders!"

Shocked and dismayed Mack asked, "Are you ordering me to go see a shrink?"

The Chief leaned forward and hissed, "I am ordering you to seek professional psychiatric counseling."

Not fully believing this was happening to him, Mack asked, "On what grounds is this order being made?"

"On the grounds it is my professional opinion you should take a proactive approach to emotional health for your safety and the safety of the men you supervise, and to ascertain that you are emotionally and psychologically fit to continue your command," the Chief loudly replied.

Mack felt deep in his heart that hell would freeze over before he would open that box in front of a non-firefighter, much less a shrink. Knowing full well he was staring down the barrel of a loaded gun Mack stated, "With all due respect, Chief, I am not a threat to myself or my crew. I am and will continue to be a damn good officer. I will not go see a psychiatrist."

He got the stare again, and Mack thought, *Damn, I hate that stare.*

Big Al reddened again and said, "Lieutenant, are you disobeying my direct order?"

With his back against the wall and a firm conviction, Mack replied, "Yes, sir, it looks like I am."

The game was finished. The Chief stood up and as Mack stood to leave, Big Al ordered, "Stay seated, I will be back in a moment," and he left the office.

Mack sat there in the, by now, very uncomfortable chair and wondered to himself, *What in the world just happened?* He had never in his career disobeyed an order. At this moment, though, he had zero respect for Big Al Fuentes and zero respect for his uncalled for order. Mack was in self-preservation mode and was confused as to what would happen next.

In the outer office, Mack could hear the chief mumbling to his secretary and the frantic clicking of a keyboard. The printer in the Chief's office came on and it spit out a sheet of paper. Mack stared at it, knowing what it could be.

Chief Fuentes came back in his office and grabbed the paper from the printer as he sat down in his big chair. Having composed himself slightly, he asked Mack, "Have you reconsidered your decision?"

Mack, not so defiantly said, "Sir, I stand by my decision."

The Chief slid the paper across the desk to Mack and said, "Okay, Lieutenant, read and sign this form."

Mack's body deflated as he read the following on official Stephenville Fire Department letterhead:

Lieutenant Peyton McWhirter,

Effective immediately you are suspended from active duty with the Stephenville Fire Department for a period to be determined by the Chief of the Department. The basis for this suspension is for the following infractions:

1. Failure to obey lawful orders
2. Insubordination
3. Conduct unbecoming an Officer

Furthermore you are barred from wearing any part of the Fire Department uniform and from entering any Fire Department property on a non-emergency basis. You will be contacted by the Chief of the Department upon termination of this suspension or termination of employment.

Alexandro Fuentes, Fire Chief

Mack's eyes went from the paper to the big greasy haired man leaning back in his big chair. This time it was Mack's turn to stare. When he saw Big Al lose the staring contest and start shifting in his chair he asked,

"Chief, why are you doing this?" as he signed his order of suspension.

The chief responded with a hint of gloat in his voice, "Lieutenant, I run a modern Fire Department in modern times. I have had extensive training to do this. When I render a professional decision, I expect it won't be questioned and I expect my orders to be carried out to the letter. Your time off will allow you to think about your decision today."

Then the Chief added, "That will be all."

Mack stood, turned and left the office in a daze. He did not see all the eyes of the second floor on him as he descended the stairs. He couldn't hear the murmuring in his wake.

Mack entered the property room exactly at the punch line of one of Doug's jokes. Everybody was knee slapping and laughing, but he couldn't hear it. He just kept walking to the other door. His crew stopped laughing, and gave each other confused looks. They fell in behind their officer and filed out the door. They boarded the engine in silence but it was too much for Bear, and he tried to break it with, "Hey, Loo, I got that cap from Doug for you."

Mack stared straight ahead, let out a big breath of air and said, "I guess I won't be needing that. Big Al put me on indefinite suspension."

After a short shocked silence, the driver and fire-fighter both lit into it with, "That sunuvabitch, he can't do that!" "We'll fix this, blah-blah-blah." Mack heard none of it and sat in silence, just staring at the road with the tunnel vision of a man in shock.

When they arrived at Station 7, Mack called a table meeting and told the crew what had transpired in the Chief's office. When he told them what the basis for the suspension was, they all got irate, calling it stupid and senseless. They all understood what really needed to be done for healing.

Mack told them to not be too vocal about it and advised them, "Boys, I think there is a storm headed your way too. If Big Al offers any assistance, I would recommend you take it. But be careful about letting that shrink get in your head." He looked around the table then added, "If you want to talk, I reckon I'll be easy enough to find in the saddle shop."

About that time, the officer relieving Mack arrived. Lieutenant Williams looked Mack straight in the eye and extended his hand saying, "I'm sorry to hear it, brother." Mack shook his hand and thanked him. He treated it as a normal shift relief telling what they had done, which wasn't much, and what needed to be done. He added, "Make sure somebody writes a memo about that coffee table."

As he was cleaning out his locker, Mack thought, *I don't need half this stuff.* But he saved it all. He loaded it all in his truck and fired up the old Chevy, but just sat there. He didn't want to leave, especially under these circumstances. He was a fighter, but right now the fight was over. He would leave, beaten. As he pulled around the front of the station to hit the road, he saw his whole crew standing at attention in front of engine 7. As he passed by, they all saluted.

CHAPTER 4

I'm Okay, But I Wonder About You

"We are not going to stand for this crap!" yelled Bear as the crew filed back into the station. He had been on the job 30 years and had opinions about everything fire department related. Everyone usually deferred to his rants so they wouldn't have to argue with him. His debate tactic was to be loud, insistent and annoying. "I'm getting on the horn with our association president and let him know what happened, this just ain't gonna fly! There's going to be an investigation! That fat bastard can't do this!" Everyone certainly agreed. They were riled up and this just put more wind in his sails.

He went into the office to make his call and the guys out in the day room could hear him easily. He was telling the association president what had happened and what Mack had said about them probably being next. Bear was demanding an investigation to start right away. The president asked if he was on a fire station phone and he said yes. The president warned, "Don't say anything else and don't discuss this with anyone on any fire station phone, even if they call you wanting info."

The surprised driver asked, "Are you saying our phones are bugged?"

The response was, "It's been known to happen and I wouldn't put anything past this Chief. I'll be out there in a little bit."

Bear came out of the office and told everyone the Prez would be out to talk to them and to stay off the bugged phone. He emphasized this point because he always enjoyed a good conspiracy theory. The Lieutenant who came in to relieve Mack just sat back with the new rookie and let the crew go at it with all of their theories and complaints. The last thing he wanted was to have them turn on him. He didn't want to be branded a chief sympathizer for trying to interject common sense. They were all mad and he thought it best to let them vent.

In about an hour, Jim Bob Thomas, the president of the Stephenville Professional Firefighters Association, came in the station and had a seat. The riled up crew jumped in with both feet. He let them go a while until they got tired of talking.

"What the Chief has done is not against the law. It was not a smart move but it's not illegal. The association will address it with him and work our contacts with the mayor and city council to see if we can get the problem rectified. In the mean time, if anyone is ordered to go see a shrink I would recommend you follow that order. If any order is given you are bound to follow it. This is not to say if you have to go to the shrink that you have to be direct with your answers. Do not go in mad and do not incriminate yourself in anyway. These guys talk in circles to confuse you; maybe you should heed that and speak their language. Understand what I'm saying?"

One of the regular guys at the station asked, "Just what *are* you saying?"

This fired up old Bear again and he hollered, "You just aren't the sharpest knife in the drawer, are you? He is saying talk all around the question, make a lot of noise but don't answer it. Talk in circles, boy! And for goodness sake, don't tell him about that time you went camping with your Uncle Wilbur in Arkansas or how your mother breast fed you till you were twelve!"

Jim Bob laughed and said, "Yeah, some of that is what I am saying, don't give him any ammunition. We are going to watch what is going on, so if anything happens ya'll give me a call to keep me updated. If you get called down to the chief's office, let me know and I will go with you."

Jim Bob left and Lieutenant Williams reminded the guys they were firemen and not members of Aunt Emma's quilting club. "So quit the gossip and speculation and get on with the fireman stuff." They were way behind on the day's duties, so everyone got busy. The drivers were checking out the equipment and filling out the checklists. The firefighters hit the house duties. While everyone was hard at it, the Battalion Chief pulled up in his fire department suburban. He came in the station with all eyes on him. He passed the Lieutenant and he said, "Let's go in the office."

The two officers went into the office and closed the door. There is nothing like a closed door in a fire station to get the curiosity going. Everyone got as close as they could to try to catch anything that was said. One of the medics even went and got his stethoscope to use on the wall.

The Batt Chief opened with, "I could have called but I didn't think that would be right. I'm not sure what is going on but the Chief told me to get the guys that were at the Crabtree fire with Mack down to the psychiatrist's office on Oak Street. Ya'll take the engine down there. I guess you will just be an innocent bystander since you were not at the fire. If they refuse to go then I am to relieve them of duty and take them to see the Chief." He appeared very uncomfortable carrying out his orders. He continued, "I wanted to tell you that in private so you could handle it as you see fit. Now, I have to talk to the whole crew. Let's round them up."

The crowd by the door quickly scattered.

The Lieutenant got on the intercom calling everyone up front. The only one not there was the new firefighter. He was cleaning the bathroom. When the group was assembled, the Batt Chief started, "Guys, I am just carrying out orders and I have no explanation, so save your breath. Chief Fuentes has issued a non-discussion order for this entire crew. You may not discuss anything about the Crabtree Ranch fire with anyone other than yourselves. Say nothing to anyone outside of this crew. If it is found out you have said anything, then official charges will be levied with penalties up to suspension." He looked around the room for effect then said, "That is all I have to say. Are there any questions? And like I said, I know nothing."

The room was silent. They knew no explanation would be given so they just stared. "Okay. I'll see ya'll later. Be careful." He left the station thankful they were leaving it alone.

When he had driven away, the conspiracy theories and accusations started in high volume. The officer interrupted the discussion telling his engine driver and the guys on the ambulance about the Chief's orders. They needed to leave for the shrink's office right away. "Ya'll remember what Jim Bob said because it starts now. This stuff is getting serious."

When they got to the office on Oak Street, the Lieutenant told dispatch on the radio they were on limited response so the interviews wouldn't be interrupted. They checked in with the receptionist. She seemed to be tickled to have her regular day broken up by a room full of good-looking firemen to flirt with. It was a great opportunity but the men were not in much of a flirting mood, she was let down they wouldn't play the game.

The first to be called back was the old driver, Bear.

Bear walked into the shrink's office and was met by a small man with narrow shoulders and a funny haircut. He had a voice like some actor on a TV comedy show. Bear did not like him. The Doctor introduced himself "Hello, I am Dr. Wilbarger." Silence. "And you are?"

"They call me Bear."

"So, Bear, what is your full name?"

"Bear will work. I'm sure you have the rest of it on some paper somewhere."

"Um, well, yes I do. Bear, how are you today?"

"Oh, I'm fine. Thanks for asking."

"That's good. Bear, we are here today to talk about a fire you were involved in."

"Which fire? I've been to a lot of them."

"Well, the fire that claimed the life of your fellow firefighter."

"Okay."

"So, how do you feel about that?"

"How am I supposed to feel?"

"Oh, um, well I've never lost a work partner so I can't say."

"But you are the professional on feelings so I am asking you how am I supposed to feel."

"Um, well, sad, depressed, remorseful, I would think."

"Okay."

"So how are you dealing with it?"

"With what?"

"Your loss. You do count this as a loss don't you?"

"Oh, well, I deal with it by going to work."

"Is that all? Do you have any other coping mechanisms? Do you have anyone to talk to? Any close friends?"

"I talk at work."

"Do you find yourself drinking heavily or relying on drugs?"

"No, do you think I should?"

"Oh, um, well. Certainly not. That would be an unhealthy crutch."

"I agree. I don't know why you would even suggest that."

"I did not suggest that. I was asking."

"Whatever you say, Doc."

"Let's leave that subject a minute. Can you tell me about your family life?"

"I'm single."

"What about growing up?"

"My mom was killed in a domino game when I was three. My dad ran off with a two-bit whore a year later. I was raised by my grandparents on a goat farm."

"Would you say you had a happy childhood despite your loss?"

"Yeah, I like goats. They are funny to watch."

"Did you miss your parents?"

"Never knew them, so I guess not."

"Bear, how do you view death?"

"It's pretty final and nobody gets out alive do they? How do you feel about it?"

"This isn't about me, Bear. I'm here to help you."

"Like I said, I'm fine. Or am I? Do you see a problem I should be aware of?"

"I can't say, Bear. I've just met you."

"Well, if you see any red flags would you let me know? I try to keep myself physically and mentally pure, so if you see a problem let me know."

"So, Bear, you talk about things at work. Do you find yourself on edge more than normal?"

"I'm always on edge. And speaking of work, I need to get back. Our engine is out of service while I'm here. Are we through?"

"Well, I'm not sure if we are through or not. I guess that would be up to you if you have nothing else to share."

"Well then, I guess we are through. Nice to meet you, Doc." With that, Bear got up and left the office.

The next in line was one of the paramedics. After the greetings and handshakes he had a seat. Dr. Wilbarger opened the same way. "We are here today to talk about a fire you were at."

"Yes, sir. If there was a fire I was probably there."

"This was the Crabtree Ranch fire where a firefighter was killed."

"Yes, sir. I was there."

"I understand you were one of the paramedics attending to the injured firefighter."

"Yes, sir."

"How do you feel about that?"

"I did all I could."

"With the outcome I would think there might be room for self doubt. Would you say that could be a problem?"

"I did all I could."

"I understand. How do you feel about the fire service?"

"I do all I can."

"Would you say the fire service is good to you?"

"Yes."

"I see. Are you married?"

"Yes."

"How is your home life?"

"I do all I can."

The shrink was getting pretty frustrated by all this and didn't want to continue to waste his time. He knew it would take a long time to crack these nuts, if he ever could. "Hmmm, you seem to be a vigilant man in respect to your responsibilities. I'm not sure we are going to get very far today. Do you have any questions?"

"No, sir. Are we through?"

"I think we are. Have a nice day."

The firefighter/paramedic left and joined his crew back at the truck. The men were satisfied they'd carried out their orders to go see the psychiatrist and it was over. They spent the rest of the shift psychoanalyzing one another.

CHAPTER 5

Back to the Scene

After he left the station, Mack drove around without a destination, just looking at the country. He was in a daze. He didn't have any particular place in mind but he didn't want to go home to the Dead Dog Ranch. He didn't want to go to his saddle shop either, even though he needed to.

He knew in his heart what he really needed to do was figure himself out. He tried to be objective and ask himself the questions he would ask someone else. He had never disobeyed an order before; he always respected the rank, if not the person. He was angry with himself. *It's probably going to cost me my job.* It was a job that he loved dearly. The thought of talking to a psychiatrist angered him but more so it scared him. This attitude angered him more; thinking something so simple would scare him. *Why am I so dead set against talking to a shrink?*

He drove aimlessly and questioned himself into a very dark place. Someplace he had not been in a very long time. The first fire.

Much later, Mack's eyes were full of tears as he drove on and thought of the things he'd been hiding from himself all these years. The things he hid in that box in his mind. He thought now how it felt for the weeks after, back then. The guilt of not being able to save them and the soul crushing sense of loss had become too much. He tried to drown the memories in whiskey but they learned how to swim — he could not escape that day.

On one drunken night he'd driven out to the fire scene, which had at one time been a happy place, and walked to the back of the property to a stock tank. He had his pistol in his back pocket. He thought about how he sat on that tank and pondered what life seemed like it was going to be. To him at that moment the future seemed as dark as his thoughts.

He prayed to God to forgive him for what he was about to do. He cocked the hammer of the Ruger .45 long Colt and placed it to the side of his head. He hoped one bright flash of light would take the darkness away. As he put his finger on the trigger, a strong nudge from behind knocked the gun away from his head. He turned to see a buckskin-colored horse behind him staring at him. He hollered to scare the horse away but it wouldn't leave. He fired the gun and the horse spun and ran into the darkness.

Mack sat back down and again picked up the gun. Again, the horse returned and nudged it away. Mack fired the weapon again, and the horse ran only to come back to interrupt him again. He fired the pistol a third time, and when the horse ran into the darkness Mack stood and waited for him to return. *I'm going to take that horse with me,* he thought. The buckskin returned and walked up to Mack and just stood there, looking at him.

He placed the barrel of the revolver right between the deep brown eyes of the horse and tightened his finger on the trigger. Click. There were only three rounds in the gun. The horse nickered and stepped forward to place his head on Mack's shoulder. As the horse rested his head there, the sun exploded over the horizon to present one of the most beautiful sunrises Mack had ever seen. He broke down and fell to his knees. In his sobs, he said a prayer of thanks to God for sending that horse and giving him this new day. A new day forever. He considered it a sign. Later that day Mack returned to the property with a trailer to get the horse, but he was nowhere to be found.

These long ago thoughts were very painful for him but Mack was thankful to remember the positive from it. He knew he would likely never tell this story to anyone. He wondered deep down if this was why he became a firefighter, to save people from the fires he hated. He didn't want anyone to be pushed to the point he had been at by a fire. He felt hopeful the sun would rise on this current problem and a sign would come.

When Mack finally got tired of driving, and figured out where he was both geographically and emotionally, he wanted to be with Samantha. As he drove to the Silver Star Cowboy Complex, where she had her training stable, he felt better. Facing that bitter memory and getting past it along with the promise of seeing Sam lightened his mood. As he pulled in the gate, he could see her working a horse in the round pen. As she took the horse around the pen in a collected lope, he said out loud, "Poetry in motion."

Mack parked his old Chevy right with all the new and shiny trucks the cutting horse boys drove. He chuckled as he slammed his hollow sounding truck door. *These boys are all about new, big and shiny,* he thought. *That's fine by me, new and fancy makes me some good money in the saddle biz.*

Mack eased on over to the round pen and waited on Sam to make another pass by. She was astride a nice looking two-year-old sorrel gelding. Mack could tell the little horse was pretty hot blooded and Sam had her hands full. She had a lot of whispering to do with this one. She pulled up and said with a half smile, "Hey, whatcha doing?"

Mack replied, "Just watching a pretty girl ride."

Sam shot back, "Well, if that's all you're gonna do, then get on that Bay horse over by the barn and ride with me. I about have the edge knocked off this one and I'm going to take him out and show him some country. I could use the company."

Mack nodded and headed toward the barn. On the way Sam hollered, "You're gonna need your spurs!" He veered toward his truck to get them.

Mack finally found them behind the seat of his truck and thought, *I haven't seen these in too long.* The spurs were handmade by a man named Wilson from down around San Saba. Mack had traded twelve sets of hand carved spur leathers for them. He considered it to be the best trade he ever made. *I ought to go see that man again now that I'm going to have some time on my hands.* It had been a long time since he'd visited the memories that darkened his thoughts this morning. Perhaps some time on the road, and a little entertainment, might keep him from dwelling on things he couldn't escape.

Mack found the Bay horse by the barn, tightened the cinch and mounted. He had ridden this horse before and knew him to be well trained and solid. Good horses were a pleasure for him. He and the Bay walked over to the round pen where Sam and the two year old were waiting. Mack side-passed the Bay up to the gate and opened it for Sam.

"Let's go down past the arenas to the back," Sam said. "I know a way to get onto Buster's place and we can ride there. He gave me permission."

Mack didn't mind riding on Buster's ranch. It was a nice place. He didn't want to go up by the house though. It was just a pile of burned wood now, but for Mack it was surrounded by ghosts. So he said, "Okay, but let's stay at the back."

Sam looked at Mack a little side eyed and said, "Sure."

As the pair rode down through the Silver Star Cowboy Complex, Mack was amazed by how much the place had changed in such a short time. A roof had been put over the cutting horse arena. Now the cutters could work their horses rain or shine. A new roping arena had been built along with a fine set of pens for the roping cattle. Mack figured team roping was getting popular because his roping saddle orders had doubled. It looked like the Silver Star was doing a good job of catering to anyone with horse and a saddlebag full of cash.

On past the roping arena was what looked like a movie set for a western town. There was a string of buildings housing a café, a saloon, a general store and a blacksmith. There were even hitching posts for the horses all along the street. Mack thought, *Throw in a few soiled dove dancehall girls, some ne'er do well gunfighters, some kids chasing stuff and the patrons of the Silver Star could pretend to be cowboys to their hearts content.* As corny as it appeared though, Mack thought it was pretty cool.

As they passed the café, out walked Bubba Crabtree. He was a big, loud man. Everyone knew when Bubba was around. He was the owner and developer of the Silver Star Cowboy Complex. Bubba was quite the western entrepreneur and had made some money on his various businesses and schemes. He was also Buster's brother. When he saw Mack and Sam, he hollered, "Hey, Mack, come on over here!"

Mack and Sam rode on over to be sociable but Sam held back a little. Sam had put Bubba in his place a few times before and didn't care for talking to the man.

Mack pulled up but didn't dismount. The two men shook hands and Mack said, "Hey, Bubba. How ya been? Looks like you have a lot going on here."

Bubba started bragging, "Mack, I've been great and yep, we have been busier than a one armed fiddle player around here. We've done a lot and got a lot more to do. I think I'm gonna put a bunkhouse at the end of town. We been getting quite a few cutters and ropers from out of town and I figger I ought to give them a place to stay. They can soak up the western ambiance, leave their horses in the barn and leave most of their money here, too."

Bubba walked closer, held Mack's horse by the bridle and asked, "What do you think about putting a saddle shop right over there by the blacksmith shop? I could make the rent affordable for ya and I wouldn't want more than 15% of the take. I tell ya, Mack, these fellas bring cash money in both pockets. It would really put you out there in front of them. I could make you famous."

Mack laughed at Bubba's "generous" offer and replied, "Bubba, I got more work than I can do now. I don't think I need to be any more famous. I'm just across the road and down a little, I don't think I need to move."

Bubba squinted up at Mack and replied, "Think big, be big, Mack. Just think of the market you would develop. Hell, now that lightning burned down Buster's house maybe that small thinking brother of mine will finally sell that 500 acres across the fence. Don't ya think a golf course would look good over there? I'm working on that, too. These rich boys like their golf and they can't ride and rope all the time. There's another untapped market for ya if you were here, boy. Lots of golf stuff uses leather."

Bubba's phone buzzing interrupted his sales pitch. The Bay horse must have thought it was a fly because he started shaking his head as if to say no. Bubba looked at his phone and hurriedly said, "Gotta go, but think about that, Mack." With that Bubba went fast stepping on up the road. Mack could still hear him talking. "Hey, Brig! Good to hear from you!"

Mack and Sam just looked at each other, turned their horses and kept riding to the gate at the back of the complex. Finally, Sam said with disgust, "Bubba blows so much smoke I'm surprised the Forest Service hasn't done an air drop on his ass."

Mack found it very attractive that she had the same disdain for blowhards that he did. As they walked the horses they made small talk, then sometimes they didn't. They didn't have to. They got onto Buster's ranch and both commented on how it was the prettiest place in the county. They were both grateful to Buster for keeping it that way.

Mack told Sam about how when the Crabtree brothers inherited the 1000 acres the Crabtree family called home they'd split it down the middle. Buster was running cows at the time, so he got the grass and water. Bubba didn't care, he was going to rape his part and build a moneymaker on it; hence the Silver Star Cowboy Complex.

"Bubba was always trying to get Buster's part but Buster wouldn't sell. He circled his wagons here. His ranch was his final stand and he meant to keep it a proper western ranch, even if he was too old to run cows anymore. His ranch house was his sanctuary and museum. The house was full of his old rodeo photos, silver trophy buckles and trophy saddles. He could sit there and happily live in his past.

"Infirmity and one last ride, just to see if he could do it, got the better of him a few weeks back," Mack continued. "He was sure he could still ride anything with hair, but he was mistaken. When he flew off a bucking horse and hit the hard ground, Buster learned he didn't bounce as well as he used to and ended up in a nursing facility in Fort Worth with a broken hip.

"Getting pulled out of his environment was really hard on him. When I visited him in the hospital, Buster had full intention on coming back to the ranch and was busy trying to talk some of the pretty nurses into coming with him. As far as I know, Buster doesn't know about the fire, it would be too much for him to take right now."

Mack was busy talking and he'd never ridden Buster's ranch before, so he didn't know where they were. He also didn't know Sam had something going on. They came out of a little tree line and over a rise and there stood the burned remains of Buster Crabtree's ranch house.

Mack sat horseback and stared at the charred pile for a minute then said, "I told you I wanted to stay—"

"I know," interrupted Sam "but you need to face this." She moved her horse up and put her hand on Mack's shoulder. "As long as I've known you, I've never seen you fear or turn away from anything."

Mack was still locked into looking at the house when she said, "I am here to help you get through this. When you are ready, we will talk."

He was surprised to think he could talk to her about it when the time came. He might even tell her about the first fire. She was not in the Fire Service, but she was in his heart.

Mack's gaze was fixed on the ruined remains. In his mind he could see the rain, the fire equipment strobe lights, the smoke, Eric's coat in front of him and the explosion. But Sam was with him and with her hand on his shoulder he felt no fear, no anxiety and no guilt. He was just replaying the events. He now knew how her horses felt when she calmed them. She was whispering and he was listening.

CHAPTER 6

Don't Take Off Your Spurs

The ride back to the barn was long and slow. His mind and emotions were in a whirlwind, and Mack was grateful for the quiet company of this amazing woman. When they got back to the barn, they unsaddled the horses and brushed them down. After putting out some feed and water, they put them in their stalls. With the day over and all the work done, Sam and Mack sat on a hay bale and had a cold beer.

Mack was just staring at his beer bottle a little too much for Sam. From out of nowhere she asked, "How long has it been since we've been dancing?"

Mack thought about it a moment and said, "Well, the last time was at the rodeo." Then added, "That was the first time, too."

"Well," said Sam, "let's do it again."

"Yeah, we ought to."

"No, dumb ass, I mean right now."

"Right here?"

"Do you hear any music here? Let's run up to the Trio Ballroom at Mingus."

"Aw, I would have to clean up and all that."

"Why? I'm not. Let's go!"

Mack mulled it over in his mind for a second and was surprised that he felt like dancing with Sam. So using one of his favorite lines from the movie *Urban Cowboy* he took a big swig of beer and said, "Get in the truck, Sissy!"

On the ride up the road to Mingus, TX in Mack's old truck, Sam admitted, "I've never been dancing at the Trio before. I've passed it when I brought horses up this way."

"I haven't been in a long time. It used to be a cowboy bar then the football team from the college took it over, then the cedar hackers ran them off. I haven't seen a cedar hacker in a long time, so I hope they're gone."

Sam giggled. "What is a cedar hacker?"

Mack explained "They are folks, mostly whole families, that travel around living in tents and travel trailers making their living by clearing cedar trees off of ranchers' land. They get paid for their labor and then sell all the cedar posts, too. Hackers set up camp on the land for the duration of the job and move on when it's finished."

Sam asked again, "So, why do you call them cedar hackers?"

Mack continued, "Oh, back in the day the only tool they used was an ax. They hacked down all the trees. Cedar hackers. I guess now they use chain saws, but maybe not. All the ones I ever met were real backward."

Sam said, "Man, what a hard life."

Mack agreed, "Yeah, and they were hard people, tough as a stump and real clannish." He added, "I heard five or six of them whipped the entire college football team and took over the bar. I guess after swinging an ax all week, whipping a football team would be pretty easy work." Mack laughed, "Friday and Saturday nights they owned the bar, but that was a long time ago."

On the way to Mingus, the couple decided they were hungry. They diverted to Strawn, the home of Mary's Café and the best, hanging off the edge of the plate chicken fried steak in the state of Texas. Mack told Sam, "During hunting season you usually have to wait an hour to get a table at Mary's."

When they finished the massive meal Sam said, "Well, I can see the reason for the wait. That was the best I've ever had. Now let's go dance it off."

After a short ride down the highway to Mingus, they pulled the old truck onto the rutted dirt parking lot of the Trio Ballroom. Those words were painted on the side of the aging concrete block and flat roofed building that was the quintessential West Texas honky-tonk. The ratty old parking lot was only half full of pickup trucks and old cars. Mack remarked, "Looks like we will have plenty of room to move tonight."

As Mack got out of the truck, he noticed he'd left the barn so fast he forgot to take his spurs off. He had his foot up on the tire when Sam walked around the truck and said, "What are you doing?"

Mack looked up, "We left so fast I forgot to take my spurs off, probably won't be needing them tonight."

Sam cocked her head a little, smiled and said, "Leave them on, cowboy. I think they are sexy."

Mack filed this little tidbit of information away for further use when the situation demanded it.

As they approached the front door, they could hear the house band doing a Merle Haggard song. *Always a good sign,* thought Mack. The Trio didn't cater to the faddish crowds like the clubs in Fort Worth. The Trio kept it real.

Both Mack and Sam enjoyed the fact that most likely the folks here tonight were cowboys, old people and oil field roughnecks. All the songs would be old country classics and had a beat that could be danced to properly.

As they entered the place, Mack could see it hadn't changed one lick. It was dark and smoky with a low ceiling. There were even some chrome and red vinyl chairs left from the '60s, the ones that had survived the bar fights. The only illumination in the place was from the stage, lights behind the bar and the extensive collection of neon beer signs on the walls. There were house lights but they were only turned on at the end of the night, usually to the accompaniment of Willie Nelson singing "Turn Out the Lights the Party's Over." Then everyone would leave the well-worn wooden dance floor and wander on home.

Mack asked Sam, "Whatcha having?"

She smiled and replied, "How about a Shiner Boch."

"I'll be right back," and Mack was off to the bar.

Sam found a table against the wall right under the Hamm's Beer sign, the one with the bear on it, and staked her claim. Mack brought back the beers and they sat and soaked up the beer and the music. Sam talked about how she loved these old honky-tonks in Texas. She said she thought Texas was calmer compared to the other dancehalls she'd been to in other states. People seemed to have better manners here or maybe you just got your butt kicked quicker if you got out of line.

The band started taking a shot at Gary Stewart's "Whiskey Trip." It wasn't great, but good enough to get them out onto the dance floor. That went on for the next nine songs, not great but certainly good enough to dance to. For the lucky couple, it wasn't the music but the partner.

Finally, Sam was out of breath and suggested, "Let's take a break, cowboy. I could use another beer."

Mack was glad to agree as he headed to the bar, "Beer coming up."

Sam sat at the rickety old table taking a breather and watching the old folks tear up the dance floor. She was thinking how cool it was they were still at it after all these years. Her thoughts were interrupted by a hand in front of her face, and a voice saying, "Let's dance." Sam looked up to see a college kid with a small head and a big hat smiling at her. His smile wasn't very flattering to him since he had a sorry excuse for a mustache and a dip of snuff. Sam was not impressed.

She was nice though and told him, "I just got through; I'm waiting on a beer."

Big hat drawled, "Hell, darlin', I'll buy you a beer but ya gotta dance with me."

Sam didn't smile when she said, "I'm here with someone. Thanks, but no."

Full of alcohol and hormones, young Big Hat was up for the challenge. He sneered, "Oh, yeah? Who? I don't see nobody and even if I did, he can't dance good as me!"

Mack came up behind him just in time to hear the exchange and informed the cowboy poser, "She's with me. Why don't you just move on?"

The kid turned around and swelled up like a tom turkey when he said, "I ain't leaving till the purty lady gives me a dance!"

Mack tensed up and said more firmly now, "She's with me!"

Big Hat flexed and challenged, "Then why don't you just leave?"

He acted like he was going to rub the side of his greasy face but moved up and grabbed the brim of his hat hitting Mack square in the face with it. The move and the alcohol took the kid a little off balance. Mack recovered, saw the kid lean and took the opportunity to hook a spur behind the kid's ankle. He jerked his leg back like he was spurring a bareback horse. As the kid went down, Mack got in the air and came down on him with both knees in his chest. The kid lost his air and urge to fight with one big "Ugh!"

As Mack drew back to punch him, just to say he did, a body flew over his back and crashed into the wall right under the Hamm's Beer sign. The cowboy against the wall just piled up and lay there. Mack jumped up and spun around ready to go again when he came face to face with Gautier "Goat" Thibodaux, professional rodeo clown and a pretty good guy to know at the moment.

Goat was grinning ear to ear, he was glad to be in the fight. "Mack, that other kid was fixing to cold cock you with a longneck." With a big laugh he said, "That just wouldn't a been fair."

Sam was impressed with the whole interaction and stood up, grabbing hold of Mack's arm.

About that time the bouncer showed up with his 5-cell Maglite. He was as big as a bear at the circus but a real nice guy. He said, "Boys, I saw what happened and I'm sorry but I gotta ask you to leave and let this settle down." Gesturing at the two piles of cowboy on the floor he continued, "When they can get up, I'm going to throw them out the back door. So, if ya'll would go out the front, I would appreciate it."

Mack looked at Sam and she gave him a "what the hell" shrug. Goat said, "Come on, I got a cooler in the truck, Mack. We'll do some catching up and I promise I won't ask your girl to dance." Goat winked at Sam conveying the message "I would if given half the chance" and introduced himself. He tipped his hat and said, "Ma'am, I'm Gautier Thibodaux, professional bull fighter and guardian angel to cowboys all over the State of Texas." He smiled and said, "You can call me Goat."

The three escorted themselves out of the Trio Ballroom to the sound of Merle Haggard's "Silver Wings" playing in the background. *I sure hate to miss dancing to that song,* Sam thought as they left.

As they walked across the parking lot, Sam asked the bullfighter, "Goat, with a name like Thibodaux I guess you're not from around here."

Goat replied, "No, ma'am, I'm coon ass by birth and Texan by the grace of God. I've been a Texan for quite some time now."

Still curious she asked, "So, what brought you to Texas?"

"Well," he answered, "my family ran some cows on a little ranch down in the marshes in dear old Louisiana. It was hot, humid, muddy, and always wet. I hated that, always had. One day a gator killed my horse, bit his head almost off when he was getting a drink. Between that and the mosquitoes it was more than I could take. I packed up the pickup and drove west until I didn't see any more mud puddles. It rained on me all the way to Dallas and didn't dry up till I got to Stephenville. So that's where I stopped."

By this time, they were at Goat's pickup truck. Still listening to Goat's history, which he already knew, Mack retrieved three cold beers from the cooler and handed them out. When Goat took a breath, Mack interjected, "Back in the day, Goat was one hell of a rough stock rider, bulls and bareback horses, bulls mostly."

Goat added, "Yeah, back in the day Stephenville was rodeo central for Texas. A fella couldn't help but get involved."

Sam asked, "So, how did you get into bullfighting and clowning?"

Goat laughed and said, "I was in a slump for a while and not winning. One night at a rodeo in Eastland the clown didn't show up so I volunteered for the job 'cuz I needed the money. I was pretty fair at it so I got to thinking if I was a rodeo clown I would still be in the rodeo and I would get paid every show. That wasn't happening as a rough stock rider."

Sam said, "Well, that was pretty smart."

Goat continued, "Yeah, I thought so. A side benefit to the job, I discovered, was I could flirt with the pretty girls in the crowd as a part of my act. While their boyfriends were getting all psyched up to make their ride, I was making time with their girls."

Sam smiled, "Well, aren't you the player? Didn't that get you into a lot of fights?"

Goat grinned and answered, "Sometimes, if I made a miscalculation and hit on a calf roper's girl he would try to whoop me but usually the real pretty girls were there with the bull riders. The bull riders knew if they got on my wrong side I might not be so inclined to jump in and get them out of the storm if things went south on their ride. I had a pretty good game going."

Mack cracked another beer and asked, "Where you been the last few years, Goat? I haven't been seeing you at any of the shows."

Goat pushed his hat back, tilted his head said, "Mack," and he paused, "in a moment of weakness I got married. She told me she didn't want to marry somebody that was gonna get gored by a bull, so I quit fighting bulls." Goat exhaled heavily and continued, "I went to work for that rodeo stock contractor in Odessa and had a rodeo clown school on the side. I became domesticated."

Mack shook his head and handed Goat another beer, then asked, "That's a ways off from here, what brings you down this way?"

Goat half grinned, "I'm free again and back on the road saving cowboys' asses. She left me and took my house. I heard she ran off with a bull rider from Wichita Falls."

Sam said sympathetically, "Aw, Goat, divorce is so hard and dividing stuff up is harder. I'm sorry to hear that."

Goat looked at Sam sort of funny and said, "Oh, I'm not sure if I'm divorced. I haven't signed nothing. As far as dividing property, she put my stuff in a box and left it next to the dead grass spot where the trailer was. We had a travel trailer we were living in on her folk's land and she just hooked her truck up to it and took it. I haven't seen or heard from her since."

It was quiet for a second then Goat let out a big laugh causing Mack and Sam to laugh, too. Goat added, "Hell, I like bulls better, at least you know when they are gonna hurt you."

When the laughter subsided, Goat cleared his throat and asked Mack, "I wonder, do you have a couch I could crash on tonight, Mack? I was working on a place to stay tonight when your situation came up. I had it going my way but I lost her in the crowd."

Mack was sure Sam was going to stay the night and Goat was not a judgmental guy so Mack said, "Shoot, Goat, I've even got an extra bed for you."

About that time, they could hear the Willie Nelson song start so Mack said, "Let's get on to the house, they are fixing to let out."

Goat said, "I'll follow you, and thanks for the bed."

As Mack pulled the Chevy onto the road with Goat in hot pursuit, he was thinking how good it was to run into his old rodeo clown buddy.

Sam was sitting sideways in the seat looking Mack up and down with that particular gaze. She said, "Now, aren't you glad you wore those spurs tonight?"

Mack chuckled, "Yep, they sure came in handy."

Sam smiled and said, "You jerked that punk's leg clean out from under him. I thought it was great."

As Sam popped the snaps on her plaid pearl snap shirt she murmured, "I told you I thought spurs were sexy." She slid across the seat and had her arms around him in one fluid motion. She spent the remaining miles to the ranch doing her best to distract Mack's attention from the road. Mack thought she was doing a damn fine job of it too, her calloused hands felt like velvet to him.

They arrived at the Dead Dog Ranch way too quickly for Mack. If Goat wasn't behind them, he might've just kept on driving, for a while anyway. Sam got herself put back together and they got out of the truck.

Goat pulled in behind them and as he was getting out of his truck he was hollering, "Damn, boy, you used to be able to hold your liquor better than that! You were driving slow and was all over the road!"

Mack winked at Sam, "Yeah, Goat, I guess it snuck up on me." Sam giggled.

"Well let me show you that room, Goat. It ain't much, but it beats a truck bed," said Mack attempting to change the subject.

They all went in the house and Mack showed Goat the layout then said, "I'm beat my friend, I think we are gonna hit the hay."

Goat yawned, "Me, too, amigo. This day is over for me. Thanks again and I'll see ya'll in the morning. Good night, Sam."

Sam smiled, "Goodnight, Goat, I was glad to meet you tonight."

Mack and Sam went to his room and closed the door. They undressed each other and fell into bed. They snuggled under the old patchwork quilt Mack's mom had made and both were thankful to be holding each other tonight.

CHAPTER 7

Answers on the Road

Morning came with the rising sun and all three friends were on the porch to welcome the new day. Mack and Sam were pretty chipper because they woke up together. Goat was happy because he woke up in a bed alone. He certainly enjoyed the process of getting and keeping a bed for the night but he didn't relish the awkward exodus that he had to go through in the morning. Sometimes, it involved jumping out of the bedroom window just as the man of the house got home after working the night shift. This morning he just got up, went into the kitchen for a cup of coffee and wandered out onto the porch to be with friends. He liked the simplicity. But then, too, he enjoyed the company of a pretty girl in the morning so he engaged Sam in conversation.

"Sam, you heard all about me last night, but what about you?"

Sam put her coffee cup down and said, "Well, Goat, I ride horses. That's about it."

Mack chuckled as he watched the two. He knew it was two opposites meeting in the middle. Goat wanted conversation and Sam wasn't much on small talk.

Goat asked, "Where are you from?"

"I was born on the Rosebud Reservation in South Dakota. My family broke horses up there."

Evidently Goat was not used to pulling words out of women. He stared at her, slack jawed, and pressed, "And?"

Sam said, "And what?"

Goat kept on, "What brought you down this way?"

"Well the way you felt about mud? I felt the same way about snow and cold." She casually took a drink of coffee and continued, "I was pretty good with horses so I started heading south working on ranches. If it snowed or the cowboys wouldn't leave me alone, I just headed south some more. When I was in New Mexico I heard the cutting horse business was big in Texas and there was some money in it, so here I am."

Goat tilted his head back and looked at Sam a moment then said, "That is pretty dang impressive that a purty girl such as yourself worked on ranches all the way from South Dakota to here. Would you marry me?"

Sam considered Goat a friend now and not a threat so she smiled and said, "Well, Goat, you are already married if I remember correctly."

Goat hung his head and mumbled, "My past continues to haunt me." He laughed a little to himself.

Sam laughed. "Enough of these proposals, I have horses to feed. Mack, can I borrow your truck to get to the barn?"

Mack smiled at her. "Sure you can. Goat will run me up there after we solve all the problems of the world here." Mack got up to give her the keys and a kiss, too. "I'll see you later."

The two men watched Sam drive off down the driveway and Goat remarked, "She's a goodun', Mack."

Mack agreed. "She sure is."

Goat broke the trance with, "Hey, we got anymore coffee made?" He went in the house to find out. He hollered back out to Mack, "You still fighting fires and saving lives?"

As Goat was walking back out to the porch, Mack was thumping his can of Copenhagen on the heel of his boot. "Well," said Mack as he packed a dip of snuff in his lip, "as of a few days ago I'm not. I got suspended."

With shock and surprise on his face Goat exclaimed, "What the hell? Why?"

Mack didn't want to start the day with it but reluctantly said, "I was involved in that fire over at Buster's place and a firefighter got killed. The chief was trying to force me to go see a psychiatrist about it. I refused and he put me off to reconsider." With that Mack got up to get another cup of coffee, signaling to Goat that was all he wanted to say about the subject. Mack didn't want to hear what Goat thought he ought to do or what Goat would do.

When Mack came back out on the porch, Goat said, "Well, I don't blame you for not going to see a shrink. I don't trust those guys one bit. If one of them got into my head it might scare him to death. Shoot, the only thing in there is naked ladies and bucking bulls anyway."

Mack laughed, "Yeah, you've always been one to keep it simple."

"I have found that simple is a good way to go. What 'cha gonna do now?"

Mack pushed his hat back on his head. "Hell, I don't know. I guess stay busy in the saddle shop and wait to see how it all pans out."

Goat remembered that he needed some repairs done and said, "Speaking of the saddle shop, do you think you could knock out some quick sewing repairs for me?"

"Sure, let's run by the shop on the way to get my truck. You ready to go?"

Goat didn't answer. He just got up and went to the truck so Mack followed.

As Goat fired up the old Ford, instantly the George Jones CD in the player started blaring "He Stopped Loving Her Today." Goat turned it down as he commented, "Nobody can sing them like Old Possum."

As the two friends drove down the road to town, Goat remembered, "It's funny you should mention Buster's house burning. That's why I'm in town. When I heard it caught fire, I headed this way to see if I could help. You knew we used to rodeo together, didn't you? When I got to town, I went out there to his place to see him. His kids were out there and told me he was in a rehab in Fort Worth nursing a busted hip from getting bucked off a horse. I didn't know that had happened. That crazy old fart, he should have known he was too old for ill tempered horses."

Mack agreed, "Well, I guess we all wonder if we have one more ride in us."

Goat continued, "His kids said they hadn't told Buster about the fire yet. That was probably a good thing, too. They said they were out there to salvage anything they could for him before the city bulldozers pushed it all down. Bull Hockey!" Goat was agitated now. "Mack, they were going through those ashes like a pack of coyotes over a cow carcass. They were arguing and fighting trying to find Buster's gold and silver trophy buckles. And he had a lot of them, too! He even had some solid silver loving cup trophies from Madison Square Garden rodeos from when they used to award those! Solid silver! Those little bastards were digging and fighting and I bet they were headed right straight to the metal buyers after they left the ranch."

Goat calmed down for a minute and continued, "I knew the old fart had kids scattered all over and they weren't close, but that was just sad. I left there to go see him in Fort Worth but it was late so I went to Mingus instead."

Mack said, "Yeah, I need to go see him, too. You said there were bulldozers from the city there? That's strange."

"Yeah, they said it was a hazard. I'm gonna go see him this afternoon. You want to go?"

Mack thought that Sam would like to go see Buster also, so he said, "Not today, I want to take Sam when I go. He likes her. I think she has a full day today, so we will go later. When you go, be sure not to mention the fire. That was all he had in this world, his museum out there. It might just kill him. We should wait 'till he is stronger and not so busted up."

As they pulled up to the saddle shop, Goat said, "Yeah, you are right. Hell, I don't know where he will go when he gets out. Maybe one of those kids will show some sympathy, but I doubt it." As Goat got out of the truck he was muttering, "Little bastards."

Mack got out of the truck and went to unlock the door to the shop. Goat was right behind him. As they entered, Goat exclaimed, like everyone else that came into the shop. "Man, I sure like the smell of a saddle shop! There ain't nothing like it."

Mack thought all he could smell was a lot of hard work staring at him. He gave Goat the basic shop tour, showing all the leather machines and hand tools, some of them antiques but still in use. The rolls of leather were all in the storage rack by the cutting table. There was a side of leather laid out on the cutting table with patterns scattered all over it waiting to be cut. Mack moved one of the patterns and the leather underneath it was a lighter color. Vegetable tanned saddle leather will oxidize and darken when exposed to sunlight. Goat knew this piece of leather had been laying out for quite a while. When he saw it, he mentioned, "Not exactly setting the woods on fire making saddles, are you?"

Mack embarrassingly replied, "No, Gladys went down and I had to work on her and then all this other crap happened. I just got no wind in my sails, man."

Goat raised his eyebrows, "Who is Gladys?"

Mack pointed to the big black behemoth of a harness-stitcher. It was a Union Lockstitch needle and awl machine made in 1952, according to the serial number. It had been rebuilt numerous times, but being built of cast iron it just refused to wear out. It was an industrial machine built to run hard all day every day. Mack had thought about trading her in on one of the new single needle machines but he liked the old ways and enjoyed hearing the chinka-chunk, chinka-chunk sound it made when it was sewing.

Mack explained, "I call her Gladys because these machines are like women. When they are running right, they are great, but then they will get cantankerous on you for no apparent reason. They are very temperamental. Most shops only let one person sew on the machine. I swear this machine can read my mind. So, I guess I call her Gladys because I say, I'm Gladys running right today."

Goat laughed as he looked at the four saddles in various stages of completion. The leather on saddles is worked wet so while one is drying the saddle maker will be doing another procedure on another saddle that has dried. Progress on each saddle is staggered to keep the work flowing. But the flow had stagnated in Mack's shop.

Goat remarked, "It looks like you got a lot done and have plenty to do." He had moved to Mack's bench now and was inspecting all the hand tools. "So you're saying you just lost your give a shit?"

"That's pretty much it, Goat. I like the work but I just don't care to do it now."

Goat kept inspecting and testing the edges on knives. He said, "Mm... hmm...." After a few minutes he said, "Ya know, the same thing happened to me when that damn woman took my house and left me homeless. My head was somewhere else for a while. I always told the students in my school if your head ain't in the game, then the rest of your body shouldn't be in the arena. I heeded my own advice and quit for a while. Hell, I could have got killed or worse. Bulls ain't very forgiving of mistakes."

Goat turned to look at Mack, he leaned against the bench and continued, "So, I took that box of stuff she left me, bought a case of beer and headed down to the Big Bend to sort things out in the desert. Remember that artist we know named Read? He has an old adobe hut down there, so I just holed up there for a while till I had it all figured out. I came back a better man, or at least as good a one as I can be. Maybe you ought to go off somewhere for a while."

Goat started whittling on a piece of leather with one of the razor sharp knives. He added, "Call Read and see if that adobe is available, there are some fair señoritas in Lajitas that will be nice to you, too."

Mack pondered what Goat had said for a few minutes then said, "That's not a bad idea, Goat. It's not like I'm getting anything done here and the fire department didn't tell me I had to stay close."

"Well, I tell ya, it worked for me. And speaking of going somewhere, if I'm gonna see Buster I better get headed to Fort Worth. Can you stitch up my gear bag real quick?"

Mack made quick work of the sewing job and the two friends were back in Goat's truck headed to the Silver Star Cowboy Complex. When Goat drove through the gate he remarked, "This place is a damn disgrace."

They pulled up to Mack's truck and before he got out Mack leaned over to shake Goat's hand saying, "Thanks for the advice, Pard, and thanks for saving my ass last night."

Goat smiled and said, "That's what I do, man."

Mack got out of the old Ford, slammed the door and Goat drove away. He didn't know when they would meet again but he sure was thankful for old cowboy friends.

Mack found Sam in the back of the barn busting up some hay bales, getting ready to feed the horses. As he was getting his keys from her he asked, "Could you come by tonight after you are through?"

She smiled, flipped her raven black braided hair over her shoulder, looked at him side eyed and bargained, "Yeah, if you cook me dinner."

Mack played along, "We are having steak on the grill then."

She stood and looked him straight in the eye now and asked, "Something up?"

Mack replied, "Aw, I just want to talk about some stuff."

CHAPTER 8

Going

After Mack returned to the ranch after seeing Sam and sat on the porch for a long time. He pondered his situation until he arrived at a decision about which path to take. When he was comfortable in his mind with his decision, and uncomfortable with sitting, staring and thinking, he got off the porch to start the fire. He went into the house to get a beer because BBQ fires always start better when you have a beer in your hand. As he came back outside he saw Sam's truck coming up the drive. Mack turned around to get her a beer as well.

Sam stopped her truck beside Mack's and got out. He could see, as she walked toward him, her Wranglers were ripped from her thigh all the way down. He laughed, since she wasn't limping, and said, "It looks like you could use this," and handed her the frosty beer.

Sam replied with exasperation, "You were reading my mind." She took the beer and turned it up.

Mack asked, "What happened?"

"Oh, I just got into a little storm with that two year old I'm riding." She pulled her pocketknife out of her pants pocket and sat on the edge of the porch. As Mack stood there big eyed, she pulled off her boots and her jeans. Mack was glad he lived far from neighbors. Sam opened her pocketknife and cut the legs off her pants and put her new cut-offs back on. She said, "I needed some new cut-offs anyway." She turned her beer straight up, drained it and said, "That bottle had a hole in it. You need another?"

"No, I'm good." Still laughing and shaking his head, he said, "I gotta start this fire."

"Well, I'm thirsty," Sam headed back into the house.

As Mack was getting the fire going, Sam came back outside wearing one of his old fire department tee shirts. The Maltese cross on the left chest had a most appealing jiggle to it. Carrying her fresh beer she came and stood by Mack watching the fire. In a minute she asked "Did Goat leave?"

"Yeah, he was headed up to Fort Worth to see Buster. It sure was good to see him again, especially under the circumstance at Mingus."

Sam laughed. "Yeah, he came in mighty handy there. He seems like quite a character. How long have ya'll known each other?"

Mack said, "Aw, I don't know, twenty years maybe. He was clowning when I started rodeoin'. We hit it off and have been friends ever since. We seem to run into each other here and there and pick up where we left off, one of those kinds of friends." Mack started in on all the past stories on Goat. The man, the myth, the legend.

"I don't want to interrupt but are we going to eat tonight?"

Back on task, Mack exclaimed, "Oh, yeah! I'll go get those steaks, that fire is past ready." He ran into the house and returned with some fine cuts of meat and two ears of corn that had been soaking. Mack put everything on the grill and closed the lid. He asked her, "How about another cold one?" When he returned with the two cold bottles, he handed one to Sam.

"Thank you," said Sam. After a moment, Sam finally asked, "So, what's on your mind? You said you wanted to talk?"

Mack had switched gears in his mind from the thinking on the porch to stories about Goat. Sam in her cut offs and T-shirt didn't help his thought process, either. He quickly organized his thoughts and got evasive. "What are those steaks looking like?" He opened the grill and flipped the steaks and corn then said, "It looks close."

Sam looked at him with that stare.

Mack confessed, "Well, I'm spinning my wheels trying to work in the shop. That fire at Buster's place and Eric getting killed is eating me up. Usually we work out that stuff at the station but none of the guys have tried to contact me and I'm barred from going up there to the station. The fire department didn't tell me I had to stay close by and I'm just in a bad spot here. I wanted to tell you I'm going to hit the road for a while to figure things out."

Sam understood his situation and agreed. "I think that would be a good idea. A change of scenery would do you some good. Do you have a destination in mind or just going traveling?" She said this against her personal desires; she was beginning to enjoy the increased time they spent together.

Mack said, "I think I'll take the long way to Port Mansfield where we all go fishing. I have plenty of friends along the way I need to catch up with. There is a retired fireman I know that runs a guide service down there. I'll just stay with him for a while."

Sam knew she had no ropes on Mack but was concerned when she asked, "So, when are you coming back?" She had begun to realize she was more attached to this man than she knew, but she didn't want him to know it.

Mack replied, "I guess I'll be back whenever I come to grips with that fire or when and if the fire department calls me back in."

The wind shifted and blew the grill smoke over them and Mack exclaimed, "Dang! Let's eat." Mack pulled the food off the grill while Sam ran in the house for plates and two fresh ones. The couple sat on the porch and ate the meal, while Mack talked about all the people he could visit with along the way.

Sam could sense his excitement about it and thought it would be good for him to go. She just couldn't shake the feeling that Mack was not himself. Something was there she couldn't touch or explain. It was more than this fire, more than being given time off. Sam knew Mack wouldn't take kindly to her poking into his psyche, but it was her gift to sense when animals were damaged. Mack was most definitely damaged.

With the meal finished and all the words spoken, they sat on the porch in silence. As it got dark, Sam broke the silence by asking, "So, when do you plan on leaving?"

Mack turned, looked at her and announced, "I guess I will hit the road in the morning."

CHAPTER 9

Only One Reason to Stay

The morning sun coming through the window found Mack and Sam still in the bed. Neither one was very acquainted with still being in bed when the sun came up; they were up before the sun people. Passionate preliminary goodbyes had kept them up till the wee hours and they were both still tired. Sam decided the horses could wait for her a little while and Mack had no particular schedule to keep. The previous night's talk of the trip had put his mind in road trip mode. He was also in no hurry to leave Sam laying warm and naked in his bed. They lay awake, silently holding hands. They both knew it might be a while before they had this moment again and neither one wanted to address that. Finally, Mack gave Sam a squeeze and asked, "How about some breakfast?"

Sam replied, "I would love it." Sam really admired the fact Mack was independent and didn't cater to gender stereotypes, besides she knew he was a better cook than her. Sam jumped out of the bed before Mack and went to the window partly to see the day, but mostly to give Mack something to think about on his trip. She stood in front of the window and Mack lay on the bed. Breakfast lost importance for a while.

Eventually, the spell was broken by growling stomachs and breakfast was made. The pair sat on the porch eating scrambled eggs, venison sausage and biscuits with apple butter. Good food and good company had them both in good spirits. Mack was thinking out loud, "I guess if I'm gonna be on the road for a while. I should run up and see Buster."

Sam agreed, "Yeah you should, he would like that. I imagine that rehab place is like being in jail for him. If you weren't starting your trip I'd like to go with you, I guess I'll try to go later in the week."

Not really wanting to part ways with her and having no schedule, Mack suggested, "Well, go with me.

I can come back through here just as easy as going down Interstate 35."

Sam was just as eager as Mack to be together but didn't want to let on, so she feigned interest in work, "Aw, I still have to feed and I want to ride the hair off that two-year old for ripping my pants yesterday."

Mack replied, "Well, a morning ride is just about gone and I'll help you feed. I'll probably give that two-year old an extra helping. I like those new cut offs."

She giggled and cut her eyes in his direction murmuring, "Oh you do, do you?" She was easing into agreement with him and said, "I guess I could give them the day off. Are you sure it won't put you out any?"

Grateful for the company Mack said, "Heck no, I got no schedule and Buster would rather see you than me anyway. He always talks about you and says he wishes he were younger."

They both laughed at that and Sam said, "Let's get going then. I'll get the kitchen cleaned up and you get packed up." Mack got his clothes packed in his old travel bag and found his tackle bag. He threw it all in the pickup just about the time Sam had the house ready to lock up. She looked at his bags in the truck. "Don't you think you are forgetting something?"

Mack looked in the back of the truck. "Nope, looks like everything."

Sam laughed. "If you're going fishing what about a rod and reel?"

Mack chuckled at her perception and explained, "They are too much trouble on a stop and go road trip. I'll just borrow Cody's. His are better than mine anyway. He builds all his own fishing rods and super tunes his reels. It will be a good excuse to use his stuff."

Not knowing what difference that made Sam just smiled, "Well, if you're ready I'm ready. Let's go feed."

"Awrighty, I'll lock up the house and meet you there."

Sam got in her truck and drove off. Mack watched her till she got to the paved road. He thought to himself he had a pretty good thing going here if he could only enjoy it without this dark cloud hanging over him. Suddenly anxious for his new adventure, he jumped up on the porch to lock the door and ran to his truck to catch up to Sam. As he ran he said to himself, "Fire Department be damned, things will get better."

When he got to the Silver Star, Sam was already half way through what she called speed feed. He helped her finish up, all the while watching her work in her cut offs and cowboy boots. She declared it finished and said, "Let's go up to the trailer so I can get some more pants on." They jumped in Mack's truck, as it was a short drive to the trailer where she lived on the Silver Star.

"Come on in, I won't be but a minute."

Mack had only been in Sam's mobile home once before and that time they hadn't even turned on the lights. This time Sam turned on the lights. She had decorated the place with Indian art and cowboy art. She had a few old saddles and other cowboy artifacts spaced around the room. The coffee table was covered with Western Horseman magazines.

Sam went into her bedroom, just off the living room, to change clothes. She left the door open and took off her clothes, once more giving Mack a memory for the road. His surroundings didn't matter at that moment. His attention was on what was framed by the doorway. Sam slowly got dressed then came back into the living room and innocently said, "Okay, I'm ready. Let's go."

Back in the truck they made their way through Stephenville. On the way they passed Mack's fire station. He tensed up as they passed by. He wondered how it was going with the guys on his shift and he was confused as to why none of them had contacted him about what had happened, he thought they were tighter than that. That and the thought of Eric's death added to his anxiety about his situation. Sam could sense his anxiety about seeing the station but didn't want to address it and fan the flames, so she acknowledged the moment by saying, "Looks like nobody is home; they must be out working."

Mack was not interested in any conversation that might bring the return of dark clouds. He replied, "Yep."

Just before leaving town, Mack noticed he was low on fuel so he pulled into the last gas station in town. Another pickup pulled in on the other side of the gas pump. Getting out of the truck was Junior, Mack's good friend and the Senior Fire Investigator of the fire department. Junior noticed Mack and hollered, "Hey, Mack. How's it going, brother?"

"Hey, Junior. How ya been? What are you up to?"

"Aw, just working. Gonna move some cows today. Man I was sorry to hear that you got put off. That just don't seem right."

"Yep, nothing right about it. How are the guys at the station doing? I haven't heard from any of my crew."

Junior replied, "There's a reason for that Mack. After you got suspended Big Al called them all in and forced them to sign non-discussion orders. I have never heard of such. They are ordered to not discuss the Crabtree ranch fire with anyone. And he ordered all of them to go for psychiatric counseling."

Mack wasn't surprised. "I told them before I left that was probably coming. How's that going with them?"

"Well, they all got their stories straight and when they go see the shrink they just talk in circles. He is so upset with not being able to get into their heads he has just about given up. He can't do anything about it with the Chief because of patient confidentiality. He don't know you can't fool with a fireman. I have spoken to some of your guys and they want to contact you but Big Al put that lock jaw order on them."

"Well, I'm glad they are raging against the machine." Mack felt better now that he knew they wanted to talk to him and he was still in the circle.

Junior got a little more serious. "So how are you holding up, Mack?"

"Aw, Junior, I'm hanging in there. I've still got a lot of figuring out to do and I have to come to terms with it all. I'm on my way to see Buster Crabtree right now, then I'm hitting the road for Port Mansfield. I thought I would do a little fishing and thinking."

"That sounds like a good idea. Salt water is good for a man. I was going to go up and see Buster to check on him and ask him about his house. I was wondering if he had any electrical problems or something that may have started that fire. A lightening strike just didn't add up for me. From what I heard from the guys that were there, it sounds like all the fire was mostly contained in the walls."

Mack thought about it a minute and agreed, "You know you are right, I went all around that house and the only fire I saw was coming out a window and a little bit out of an eave."

"Don't you think if it was a lightening strike it would have blowed a hole in the roof and some fire would show through that? That's what was bugging me."

"Yeah, even in that heavy rain I could have seen that. So what did you find out on the investigation?"

"Well, that's what I was getting at. When I asked the Chief for permission to take my department truck up to Fort Worth to talk to Buster he denied permission and told me to not talk to Buster, the case was closed. That same day was when he put the lockjaw order on your men. I went back out to Buster's place that afternoon and the city had bulldozers out there taking down the building. The operators told me the Chief had sent them out there to abate the hazard. I don't know how a burned up house in the country was a hazard. The funny thing is I never told him my suspicions; I have a few questions about this whole mess. I'm not going to let it lay."

Mack replied, "If anything important happens would you give me a call and let me know? I want to be gone, but if something starts happening I want to know."

"Sure thing brother. I will tell you now the Firefighters Association is officially questioning Big Al's tactics. Nobody has ever heard of this non-discussion order BS or ordered psych counseling and your suspension. They are even talking about getting the State Firefighters Association involved. They may be calling you. I haven't even told them what I just told you but I think I might have to."

Mack was glad he had some brothers on his side. "Well they have my number, I hope they take him down a notch. I have to get going, good talking to you, Junior."

"Good luck and bring me back some fish. Be careful and I'll see you later."

All gassed up and back on the road to Fort Worth Mack confided to Sam, "I'm glad I saw Junior and found out my guys have been ordered not to talk. I was beginning to worry about that." He went on to tell her how they were giving the psychiatrist the run around and messing with his head instead of him messing with theirs. She thought that was hilarious. Then he told her what Junior said about the fire, "Something funny is happening with this whole deal. I don't know what it is but it sure smells bad."

As they traveled northward on Highway 377 they saw the rolling grassland hills of various ranches on both sides of the road. Cattle and horses dotted the hillsides. Slowly more and more manmade structures appeared. Once they pulled through Whiskey Flats, a spot in the road populated by beer joints and liquor stores, the ranchlands were replaced by housing developments. That's the way it was all the way into Fort Worth. Traffic, houses, strip malls and people. Finally, in exasperation Mack exclaimed, "Where did all these people come from and where do they go?"

Sam agreed saying, "I don't think I could live like this. I think we take a left at the next intersection up there."

After waiting and waiting they finally made the left turn at the intersection. Up ahead they could see the place, Peaceful Meadows Rehabilitation Center. Mack laughed at the sign and remarked, "I don't think there is a peaceful meadow within forty miles of this place." He parked the truck and they found the front door.

When they went inside they noticed it to be a nice clean facility. It didn't have that old carpet and piss smell Mack was expecting. He had made plenty of ambulance runs to nursing homes and they were certainly not his favorite. There was a lot of movement all around. People walking slow and unsure and people in wheel chairs were maneuvering around in various levels of function. Four women had a card game going in the corner of the day room. As Mack and Sam approached the main nursing station a large matronly woman looked up, smiled and greeted them. "Good afternoon. May I help you?"

Mack asked, "Could you direct us to Buster Crabtree's room?"

Her expression changed just a little when she said, "That would be room 332. Are you family?"

Mack said, "No ma'am, we are friends. Has he had any family come to visit?"

Her smile left her face and she said, "Regretfully not." She then raised her eyebrows and looking directly at Samantha. She advised, "Honey, I would urge you to stay at least an arm's length away from Mr. Crabtree. He can be rather grabby."

Sam smiled, "That's Buster!"

As the couple proceeded down the hall they maneuvered around all the slow motion wheelchair racers jockeying for position in the hall. Sam took Mack's arm and held on, she was not liking this environment.

"This is spooky, Mack," she giggled nervously, but she was only half joking.

They made their way to room 332 and found Buster sitting in bed wearing a hospital gown and his beat up old Stetson hat. He was watching *Gunsmoke* on TV. He turned and saw them then hollered out, "Jumping Geronimo, if it ain't Mack and Sam!" He tipped his hat to Sam and said, "Damn, I'm glad ya'll came up this way! Ya'll have a seat."

Mack shook Buster's hand, "You look to be in fine spirits, Buster."

Sam gave Buster a hug, despite the nurses warning, and had to peel him off of her. She smiled and patted his hand saying, "Your arms are still working pretty well."

Buster laughed as he complained, "Yeah, that horse broke my ass but not my spirit. I'm getting quite the reputation with the nurses here. I'll grab one every now and then just to make some excitement. None of them have grabbed me back but I got high hopes." Buster waved his arm around the room and said, "I have been in jail cells more exciting than this place. I can't wait to get back to my ranch." He looked back at both of them. "So what's been going on back in Stephenville?"

Mack answered, "The saddle business is booming. I can't get out of the shop."

And Sam added, "I'm riding those horses daylight to dark."

Buster asked, "Are you still working out of that Silver Star train wreck my no good brother runs?"

Sam replied, "Yep, I'm still there."

Buster leaned forward toward her. "Darlin', you are good enough with a horse you ought to have your own place and not have to split training fees with that money grubbing rat Bubba."

"All it takes is money, Buster, and I don't have enough to get a place."

Buster advised, "Well get a rich boyfriend that has horses. They ought to be pretty common over there at Bubba's."

Sam made a huffing sound. "I'm not taking any of those offers."

Buster presented an offer. "Well, I've been thinking about asking why don't you move it next door on my place then? I ain't rich but I'm still good looking. I'd love to steal Bubba's horse training business away just to spite him. That sorry sucker has been trying to buy me out for a year now. He says he wants to put a golf course over there for all his rich golf playing clients. He offered me big money too but I won't ever sell to him. I'd sell it to a pig farmer before I'd let him have it. He just wants to make that train wreck bigger. I don't need his money; all I want is what I got. My house and my land. But, Sam, you are good enough and pretty enough to go into partners with. What do you think? I ought to be getting out of here pretty soon. I can't wait to get back down there and just be in my house."

Sam wasn't sure what to think. "Well, Buster, you don't have a very big barn. How could we board the horses?"

Buster scoffed, "Shoot, we will figure that out some way or the other."

Mack interrupted, "So, Buster, when do you think they will let you go?"

"I got this case worker that knows how bad I hate it here and she's working on getting me a nurse to come to the house. I hope she's a good-looking one. I figure I'll heal up a lot quicker if I have something to heal up for. The ranch would be a better place to recuperate I think, don't you?"

Mack lied, "I reckon so." Then to change the subject he asked, "Did Goat come by to see you?"

Buster adjusted his hat and replied, "Yeah, that old bull fighter came up and stayed a while. We had a good visit. The nurse I had that day was almost pretty and Goat went to work on her and it was like I wasn't here. I think it ended up she was going dancing with him that night. I don't know how that old fart does it. Sam, you stay clear of him, okay?"

Sam laughed out loud. "Oh, Buster, I already turned down his marriage proposal."

Buster brightened up at that. "Good, that means I still got a chance!"

About that time a slender German looking nurse came in the room and said, "Mr. Crabtree, it's time for your bath."

Buster replied, "I haven't seen you around here before."

She replied, "Oh, I just started this week."

Buster winked at Mack and popped his knuckles while saying, "If ya'll will excuse me it's time for my bath." He was smiling.

Mack and Sam said their goodbyes and Buster told her to keep his offer in mind. They left the room and stood in the hall for a moment, just long enough to hear the new nurse exclaim, "Mr. Crabtree, we will have none of that!"

They laughed as they navigated the halls back outside to Mack's truck. Mack drove the truck back into the traffic gauntlet of south Fort Worth. When he got past Whiskey Flats and back into the rolling hills of grass he relaxed and some color came back to his white knuckles on the steering wheel. He could talk now. He looked over at Sam and said, "Ya know, I think Buster is gonna have a real hard time when he finds out his house burned down. It sounds like his only goal is to get back there. I guess that really is all he's got, what's in that house."

Sam agreed, "Yeah, it's hard to hear him talk about that. It's sad to think what the old man will have to go through. He will have to be told sometime though."

"Yep, the right time will be a hard decision." They continued on home in silence, each was thinking their own thoughts about their friend Buster. Both felt he was too good a cowboy for what was coming his way next.

Being lost in thought on their quiet drive home the next thing they knew they were back in Stephenville. Mack's belly reminded him they hadn't eaten since breakfast. He asked Sam, "How about some dinner?"

"That's what I was thinking."

"Jake and Dorothy's?"

"Sounds good."

Jake and Dot's, as it was known to the regulars, was the same sort of café that was in every west Texas town. Simple and functional décor of wood grain Formica and vinyl covered chairs. There were photographs of past town history covering the walls. And just like every other café in Texas towns it served as the boardroom for the ranchers and dairymen of the area. Many deals were negotiated at these tables. The morning guys were usually old retired ranchers whose habit was to be up before dawn. They came for coffee and discussions of times past. After they left, the working ranchers would take a table for lunch. They discussed weather, cattle prices and the promising future. The lunch guys all addressed the morning guys as Sir. At Jake and Dot's everyone knew everyone. If someone didn't show up then his buddies would start calling and looking for him, especially the morning guys.

When Mack and Sam walked in they were met with all the howdys, heys and how ya doings. They shook hands all the way to the back where they took a table. Daisy, the waitress, came and took their order for two hamburger baskets and two sweet teas. She asked if they had heard anything from Buster and was thrilled to learn they'd just left him and was glad to get a current update on him. Rumor had it that Daisy and Buster were an item at one time but neither would admit to it.

Mack and Sam talked about Buster some. They couldn't decide the best way to break the bad news or who should do it. Both hoped Bubba wouldn't take it upon himself to go to Fort Worth and try to cut another deal while Buster was so weak. Sam said she would keep an ear open for that. Sam asked Mack again about his trip, "So what are you going to do between here and Port Mansfield?"

He sort of mapped out a rough itinerary. He presented a new idea he had been considering, "I've been thinking if Big Al won't bring me back to work then I will have more time to build the saddle business. I have about all the work one man can do."

She asked, "So how are you going to ramp up the business if you're too busy already?"

Mack explained, "I know a guy in Austin that I taught to make saddles, I think he went to work for Capitol Saddlery. I was thinking about asking him if he would come back up this way and work with me."

Sam agreed, "That would take a load off of you for sure. Do you think the Fire Department is going to cut you loose? Can they do that?"

"The Chief can do pretty much anything he wants to do and he's not a member of my fan club. I don't know what will happen. I just want to have a plan B in mind. I'm just going to explore options."

Sam asked him point blank, "Are you coming back here?"

Mack reached across the table for her hand and looked into her eyes. He reassured her, "Absolutely." The thought had never occurred to him to not return.

Daisy brought their food to the table. They were both too hungry to talk while they ate. The hamburgers at Jake and Dot's were the best around. There was no comparison between these old school hamburgers and the fast food junk that was so prevalent. They were so hungry and ate so fast they barely took time to taste the fine burgers. But they were finished and Mack regretfully said, "I guess I ought to take you back."

"I guess so."

The ride back to the barn seemed very short. When they arrived it was late afternoon and there were quite a few of the cutters on horseback working their horses. The covered arena was full of horsemen moving the cattle around getting their horses used to the action. Mack parked his truck next to Sam's at the barn. He didn't turn off the truck. He looked at Sam, "I guess I'll be back in a couple or three weeks depending on how it goes."

Sam said, "I hope you find what you are looking for." Then she slid across the seat and kissed him and held him tight. "I will miss you."

Mack whispered in her ear, "I will miss you too." They released the embrace and she slid back across the seat and opened the door to get out. She stood outside the truck and gave a little wave as Mack backed up, turned and drove away. As she watched him drive away she wondered to herself how this man had gotten so deep in her heart.

CHAPTER 10

The Road Sure Can Be Interesting

Mack decided to forgo the quick route in favor of the backroads and small town route. He was excited about leaving town and all that went with it. Now his Fire Department suspension didn't matter to him as much. He had come to grips with putting off all the saddle orders staring at him. He was glad he saw Buster again but didn't want to worry anymore about his old friend. He hoped the change of scenery would lessen his thoughts of the fires and Eric's death. The nightmares just increased his feelings of guilt. The guilt was like termites in his soul and he was having a hard time keeping his structure sound. The main goal of this trip was to kill those bugs. Sam's parting words, "I hope you find what you are looking for" resounded in his mind. He knew in his heart what he was looking for was peace and resolution. All of the problems life had handed him, he wanted to put them to rest.

As he drove the backroads he thought of Port Mansfield and how he had never had a bad time there and that is why he wanted to go. The Port was his comfort place. But twenty years as a firefighter had instilled in him the need for a contingency plan. He thought of Goat going to the Big Bend and decided to go see Stylle Read and check on the availability of that adobe, just to be safe. Anyway, it was on the way.

Mack remembered Stylle lived on Hwy 67 and figured he would know it if he saw it. He started getting into familiar country and then he saw what had to be an artist's house. The old farmhouse had been artistically modified. The large front porch was rough sawn cedar. Likewise the yard full of various cacti was encircled by a cedar stake fence. Attached at the back of the house was a boxcar from a train. On the south side was the big barn for Stylle's workspace. His specialty was western art murals. When Mack pulled up to the barn he came face to face with three huge frogs standing ten feet tall. Two were dancing and the third was playing a trumpet. They were posed like the dried frogs he remembered seeing in Mexican curio shops.

Mack got out of his truck and hollered, "Hey, Stylle!"

From back in the barn he heard, "Hey!"

In a minute out came Stylle Read wearing paint stained jeans stuffed in high top boots, a Terlingua chili cook off T-shirt and a big hat creased like Tom Mix.

Stylle saw it was Mack and yelled, "Hey, Mack, where you been?"

"Aw, down there in Stephenville, you a frog painter now?"

Stylle laughed, "Aw, these sons of bitches are just in for a touch up."

"What's the story on them?"

Stylle explained, "Bob 'Daddy-o' Wade built them for the Tango Club in Dallas a long time ago so they are called the Tango Frogs. They are sort of famous. There used to be six of them but three got burned up when they were on display at a truck stop at Carl's Corners. These three survived and I painted them up back then too. They went to a Mexican food restaurant in Nashville for a while now they are back here for a re-do and are headed to a taco joint in Dallas."

Mack said, "Man, those are some traveling frogs."

"Yeah and they will be traveling on out of here as soon as I get the clear coat on them." Stylle walked over to the refrigerator just inside the barn door and asked, "Want a beer?" He handed Mack a beer and continued, "So, what brings you down this way, Mack?"

Mack took a big swig. "I'm doing some traveling. I thought I would head on down to the coast and do some fishing but I might make it to the Big Bend, too. I was wondering if your adobe was still available. Goat said he spent some time down there."

Stylle slapped his leg, laughed and said, "Damn he did, I was down there last month and they are still talking about the crazy gringo!" He took a big draw on his beer. "Can you believe that woman just left him a box of stuff? Took the trailer and all! He came by after it happened and was pretty down. I think he rallied though; the desert was good for him. You wanting to stay there?"

"Well, if I could. I'm not sure how the trip is going to go but I might make it that far."

"Sure, you're welcome to it. Nobody is supposed to be there. If there are any squatters just run them off. You got a gun?"

"Yeah, I got one. Pard, I appreciate it. If I make it that far, do you need me to take care of anything?"

"Aw, just let me know if the place is falling down."

The two compadres visited a while and compared notes on the western art world and the saddle business. Mack decided if he stayed much longer he would be hurting in the morning. He was about four beers behind Stylle but he was getting in the mood to catch up. Finally, he said his farewells, "Bud, I need to be getting on down the road. Thanks for the use of the adobe."

Stylle said, "Sure thing man, come back when you can stay longer." They shook hands and Stylle turned saying, "I guess I gotta spray these damn frogs again."

Mack got back in his truck and headed south. As he passed through all the small towns along the way he thought back how bad it was in Fort Worth when he went to see Buster. These slower and less crowded places were so much more his speed. It was depressing, though, to see so many of them drying up.

The sun was getting lower in the sky. Mack began to think about a place to spend the night. He really didn't like driving at night, especially out here. This was deer country and they had a bad nocturnal habit of crossing the road when you least expected it. This was the country he had hunted deer in since he was young. He was going to pass by the ranch he had leased to hunt until a few years ago. Eric had been on the lease with him, he had taught him to hunt deer here. More memories. If the combination on the gate hadn't been changed he thought he could stop there and sleep in the camp house. He was still friends with the hunters on the lease and they wouldn't mind. Besides, it was off-season and the place would likely be deserted. Just before dusk he pulled up to the ranch gate. He got out of his truck and reached under the seat for his pistol. A Ruger single action in .45 long Colt. He always carried a gun in the wide-open country for snakes, hogs and such. When he got to the gate he was disappointed to see the locks had been changed to keyed locks. He said out loud, "Well, that sucks."

He returned to his truck to find out what sucked even more. The door was locked and the truck was running. He evaluated his situation and summed it up with, "Dammit!" Luckily he found some wire by the gate. He had fished it in the window and was making good progress when a ratty old pickup stopped on the road behind his truck. Two greasy vermin of wasted youth got out. The driver asked, "Got a problem, friend?"

Mack cautiously replied, "No, I locked my keys in my truck. I about got it."

"We'll be glad to help you get in that truck."

"No, thanks. I about got it."

"How 'bout we knock that window out and make it quick?"

"That ain't happening." Mack stopped working and faced them.

The greasy passenger reached into the bed of the truck and brought out an axe handle and said, "How about we just knock you out then?"

They both started moving in like a couple of coyotes.

Mack pulled out his pistol and they froze in their tracks. "How about I blow a hole in you I can throw a tom cat through?" He emphasized his point by firing one shot that took out both windows of the ratty truck. The two punks started scrambling like pigs on ice to get back into their truck. The driver got it in gear and the other one jumped in the hole in the door where the window had been. The old truck raced away in a cloud of oil smoke. Two legs hanging out the window for as far as he could see.

With the threat abated he began to feel the adrenaline pumping through him. He was shaking. This didn't make it any easier to fish that wire in the window. Just as he began to consider breaking the window the wire loop fell over the lock button and he was in. He backed the truck out onto the road and went the opposite way from Boney and Clod. Sleep was out of the question for a while.

The next town he came to he stopped at a store to get a cold drink. As he was walking out a deputy sheriff pulled in. Mack thought it would be wise to fess up to what had happened. He approached the older deputy and said, "Officer, I am a fireman in Stephenville and I might need to tell you about something that happened."

The tired old cop looked at him and asked, "What do you got?"

As Mack recounted the events the deputy became more interested. As the story progressed his eyebrows got higher and his eyes bigger.

He asked, "Was the truck an old Dodge with three colors of primer for paint?"

"Yes, sir."

"I know those bastards. Did you hit one of them?"

"No, sir, only the windows."

"Damn, you should have killed them." Then he added, "They probably won't report it but if they do I'll charge them with assault. Write down your contact info and be careful on the road, Bud." Mack wrote his name and contact info on the pad of paper the deputy had given him. The Officer took it and read it then said, "Stephenville? Didn't ya'll lose a man in a fire up there the other day?"

"Yes, sir, we did."

"Damn sorry to hear that, son. You be careful on the road tonight."

"Thank you, sir."

Mack got back in his truck and pulled out the state map to figure a route around this county. Once he got it figured out he set off for Austin. He thought he would be there in a few hours. If he could find a fire station he figured they wouldn't mind him parking in their parking lot and catching a nap. In the morning he would look up his saddle-making buddy.

Mack woke up in his truck the next morning to a tapping on his window. The Captain of the station was standing outside his door. Mack rolled down his window, "Good morning, Cap. I'm a fireman in Stephenville."

The Captain said, "Yeah, I saw your window sticker. You okay?"

"Yes, sir. I've been driving all night and just thought I would pull in here for a nap."

"Dang, boy! You want to go back to sleep or come in for a cup of coffee?"

"That coffee sounds pretty good, sir."

As the two fire officers walked into the station, the Captain asked, "Stephenville? Ya'll lost a man a while back didn't you?"

Mack reluctantly responded, "Yes, sir. I was on that fire. A backdraft got him."

"That's too bad. Was he a friend of yours?"

"He was my rookie."

The Captain stopped walking, suddenly realizing who he was talking to. He asked, "Are you Lieutenant McWhirter?"

The firefighter telegraph had preceded his arrival.

"Yes, sir, I am. Call me Mack."

The Captain knew to choose his words wisely, but what the hell. "It's a damn shame what happened on that fire. It's a bigger shame what that piss ant Chief is doing to you. The word is he put you off for not going to see a shrink."

"Yep, that's what happened."

The Captain could sense Mack didn't want to talk about it so he asked, "What brings you to Austin?"

Mack said, "Since I have some time on my hands I was going to visit a friend here on my way to the coast. I thought I would do a little fishing."

The Captain said, "Well you got a long ride, if you want to get some more rest you are welcome to one of the bunks."

"Thank you, sir, but that coffee sounds pretty good right now."

So that cup of coffee led to the Captain telling the rookies to make a full-blown breakfast. Bacon, sausage, omelets, fried potatoes and biscuits. Breakfast was full of the same jaw jacking that happens in every fire station. Firemen were all the same. Mack was stuffed and happy to be in the brotherhood. After the extended breakfast was concluded, he thanked them for the hospitality and asked directions to Capital Saddlery. He shook hands with all the crew and set out again. The Captain walked out with him. In the parking lot he told Mack, "Don't let the bastards get you down, brother."

"Thank you, sir."

When he finally got to the saddle shop he decided that Austin was worse than Fort Worth. He went into the shop and was disappointed to find out his friend, Chip Whitmire, no longer worked there. He quit about ten months ago they said, but they had directions to his house where he had his shop set up. So Mack steeled his nerves and once again entered the vortex of Austin traffic. He followed the directions to, thankfully, a less populated area on the south edge of town.

He found the address of the small frame house with a separate shop behind it. He pulled into the driveway and was met by two big loud dogs. They looked to be a Catahoula and a Pit. They acted like they were not to be trifled with and he was in no hurry to get out of the truck so he honked his horn. Chip came out of the shop and hollered at the dogs, they quieted down and ran to stand behind him.

Mack got out of the truck and spoke in an even tone so as to not alarm the guards, "Hey, Chip."

Chip was surprised and happy to see his mentor. He said, "Mack! Good to see you, man! Come on in."

The two friends shook hands and went into the shop. Chip's shop was like any other leather shop; of course the smell of leather met you at the door. Projects in various stages of completion lay piled on worktables. Finished goods hung from hooks lining the walls. Mack noticed there was not much russet colored leather in the storage racks, it was mostly black leather. Also he thought it odd, for a saddle shop, that there were no saddles in process on the saddle stands.

He jokingly asked Chip, "You quit the saddles and get into harness making? All this black leather looks like you got an Amish harness shop going here."

Chip laughed and moving his head from side to side said, "Well, I tell you my friend I'm sort of running a harness shop here. I was working at Capitol Saddlery till about ten months ago. I was the young guy and I was hungry so I didn't turn down any work there. The shop boss gave me all the non-saddle jobs. Those old guys didn't want to do nothing but saddles. I did a lot of cases, gun scabbards and strap goods. Once I got started doing it the strap goods business got pretty brisk. Mostly I worked from drawings and just figured some horse trainer had a new idea going for training aids. It was straps with a bunch of buckles, D-rings and snaps. Hell, I didn't know what it was for. I thought it was weird they always wanted black leather. Well one day a man and woman came in to talk about a project, they didn't look like horse trainers. I just up and asked them what they used this stuff for. They said it was for bondage play. Heck, I didn't know what that was. They went on to tell me how people strap each other up in this stuff and have sex. Have you ever heard of such? "

Shocked, Mack asked, "Are you telling me people tie each other up and screw? And both of them are okay with it?"

"Yep, that's what I'm telling you Bud. They said the stuff they buy in stores is cheap work and the stuff I was making was better quality and more comfortable, if you can figure that. They said word had gotten out that the saddle shop was the best place to get custom work at a good price. The shop boss was pricing it like animal harness, which don't cost too much. If he had known what it was for I don't think he would have accepted the work."

Mack said, "I ain't believing this."

"Well Mack, Austin is one of the weirdest places I have ever been. Evidently there are a lot of folks down here tying each other up; I was so busy on strap work that I didn't have time for saddles. That couple told me about the market for it and that I was doing the best work they had seen so I figured why split the money with the shop? I quit and moved it all out here. It's a tight community and people harness costs a lot more than animal harness."

Mack asked, "Have you ever tried any of it out?"

"Hell no! I may not be the best looking guy but I've never had to tie up a woman in my life."

"Well, shoot, I came by to see if you wanted to come back to work for me making saddles. But I guess you can't afford to give up your emporium of pain here."

Chip smiled. "Well, I appreciate the offer. It's weird stuff but the money sure is good."

"Well, do you know of any saddle makers looking to make a change? I'm busy."

Chip answered, "No, man, good saddle makers are getting fewer and fewer. I'll ask around though. Do you know any good strap hands wanting to work? The only people I find down here that want to learn the work, have more ink on them than the Sunday comics and have all sorts of hardware hanging off of them. They make me nervous." Then he was curious and asked, "Did you come all this way just to offer me a job?"

Mack answered truthfully, "No, I'm on my way to the coast to do some fishing. I just thought I would stop by."

"Are you still fighting fires and saving lives being a hero?" Chip laughed at his cliché.

Mack did not want to go there again today. In fact, Chip and his new business were an entertaining diversion. "Still doing that, I think, but that's a long story. Tell me more about this game you got going on here."

The more Chip talked the more Mack was amazed at what people will do. He didn't think the bondage market would go over very well in Stephenville. They laughed about it and talked about all the other gossip in the saddle making community. Mack decided he needed to get back on the road. He had about six more hours to go, with no stops. So the two friends shook hands goodbye. Chip made Mack promise not to tell the other saddle makers what he was doing now. You never knew who would jump on his bandwagon.

Mack headed south out of Austin. He was ready to be at the coast. Between traffic, gunfights, ball gags and body harnesses he was ready to be through with it. He wanted to be drinking a beer in Port Mansfield by sundown.

CHAPTER 11

Don't Mess with the Lady

The young horse Sam had been working with was coming along quite nicely. She didn't have to constantly be on the alert for a blow up with him anymore. Today she was covering some ground with him on Buster's place, just a leisurely ride. She rode up to Buster's old home place. It was just a pile of burned wood and bricks from the chimney now. The day after the fire his kids had arrived and combed the ruin for anything valuable. They came like coyotes to a fresh kill. She wondered how they knew so quickly since he wasn't very close to any of them. Who called them?

While they were there a crew from the city arrived with a bulldozer. The crew said the fire department had sent them to level it since it was a hazard. Mack had wondered about that, he said that usually didn't happen.

Staring at the pile she felt bad for Buster, she wished there was something she could do for the old man. She felt bad for Mack also, and she thought the fire must have been an awful thing to go through for him. When she slept with him she was awakened multiple times during the night by his thrashing around in the bed as he had nightmares about the event. He always woke up tired. He didn't speak much of it and even when he did, she had to make him talk. She remembered, when she was a little girl on the reservation, her Grandfather would leave for a while if he was having a bad time. He would saddle a horse and be gone. She asked him one time where he went. He told her he would go to the hills. When she asked him what he did there, he just said, "Listen." Being young she didn't understand. He told her, "Child, out there the Spirit will talk to you through the wind, the animals, the sky and the trees." She wished she knew the old ways but she didn't learn when her grandfather was here and her father had no interest in them.

Sam hoped Mack would be able to listen as he went on his trip to the coast. Hopefully he could hear what he needed and could come to terms with his burden. She wanted to be able to help him but she could go only as far as he would let her. She really didn't know how much of her help he wanted, but she knew it hurt her to see him hurt.

The young horse was getting tired so Sam headed back to the barn. She didn't want to leave the peace of the ride and go back to the activity at the horse complex. Sam figured she would get back and call it a day. Maybe run out to Mack's ranch to check on things for him and have a beer. Probably stay the night too. It was a lot quieter than her trailer at the Silver Star.

Sam rode into the barn and saw Bubba standing in the main alleyway. She dismounted and took the bridle off the tired pony. She put a halter on him and tied him to a ring on the wall so she could unsaddle him. Sam called out to Bubba, "What you doing Bubba? I don't see you down here very often."

Bubba explained, "I'm looking everything over; I'm thinking about doing a remodel on the barn. You know spiff it up a little bit. If I make it better looking I can charge more on stall rent."

"Hell, Bubba, it's just a barn."

"Shoot, darlin', appearance is everything."

Sam took this in, "Well, I just hope you don't get in my way."

"Aw it'll work out all right. Say, where is Mack? I haven't seen him around in a while."

"He went on a little road trip, going to meet some friends and talk to a guy about coming to work for him."

Bubba remarked a bit sarcastically, "Does he have so much work he needs help now?"

"He's pretty busy, I guess."

Bubba couldn't wait to offer up some new information to Sam, "I think he's probably fixin' to be less busy. I just hired a hot dog saddle maker out of San Angelo to come put in a shop here in the complex. He does some mighty fine work and he is cheaper than Mack. I gave Mack the chance but he didn't jump on the opportunity."

Sam tried to sound undisturbed, "Is that so?"

Bubba had been working his way in closer to Sam as he spoke, "That is so. Mack might not be so much in a while. No fire department job and saddle business dropping off. He may have to go looking for greener pastures." He got closer to Sam as she unsaddled her horse. "You know this remodel is going to be a big deal. I've got some high dollar investors in on it." He placed his hand on her waist. "If you play your cards right we could put in a nice apartment and you could get out of that trailer." He started sliding his hand on down to her bottom.

Without flinching at his touch she reached up on the wall and took down a quirt from a hook. She stepped back to get enough distance for a good swing and slapped the quirt right across Bubba's face. He screamed and recoiled at the sting of it, "You bitch!" He was holding the rising whelp on his cheek.

She didn't even raise her voice when she said, "You're damn right and don't you forget it. Don't you ever touch me or say anything like that again. You got that?"

"I'll kick you out of here so fast you won't know what happened!"

"You forget there are cameras all over this barn. That was all recorded. You do anything to me and I will file charges."

"Bitch, this operation is going to double in size and you ain't going to be here to grow with it! I'll be getting that land over the fence soon. It's going to be big. It won't be nothing to get a better trainer than you in here just like it's easy to get a saddle maker. Your business will dry up! You are nothing without me!"

"You ain't getting nothing, Bubba. Buster will never sell to you."

"Well now he ain't got nothing to come back to, maybe it won't be up to him. We are fixin' to start rocking and rolling around here. You better get on the train or be left behind." Still rubbing the now blue whelp he added, "You are going to have to be real nice to me to get past hitting me with that quirt." With that he turned and stormed out of the barn.

Samantha had to make about twenty trips down the alley and back to work off her fury. All the while the tied horse was looking at her like, "you gonna turn me out or what?" She finally calmed down enough to put the horse out in the pasture. Bubba's words started to sink in. She wondered what was going on that she didn't know about; evidently he had a card up his sleeve. She thought there are all sorts of legal tricks available but she didn't know how that worked. When she saw Buster last he seemed to be in his right mind so the kids couldn't pull anything. The whole thing was a mystery and she needed to keep her eyes and ears open.

Right now she would shut the barn down for the night and head on out to Mack's place. She felt closer to him there and that is where she wanted to be. Closer to Mack.

CHAPTER 12

In Safe Harbor

Mac drove. Then he drove some more. He hit San Antonio and took the loop around to avoid it. Now he was on the home stretch. Trouble was, the home stretch was a 250-mile asphalt ribbon through the mesquite brush of south Texas.

Corpus Christi broke the monotony. It was the original home of the Whataburger so he felt obliged to stop and have one, then it was back to the same view through the windshield. That was the good and bad thing about Port Mansfield. The good was it was so far not many people went there. The bad was, it was so far. All he had to do was drive and ponder his current state of affairs. He considered his situation with the

Fire Department and how he wanted to keep his job. This was a toss-up; he was pretty sour right now on his employer, if he even had one. Eric's death under his supervision was still a haunting thought. He replayed the fire over and over in his mind. It was painful but he felt this demon had to be faced. It was better to think about it while he was awake than to replay it in his dreams. The dreams were hell. They were worse than the fire itself.

He was snapped out of his dark thoughts by a blur in front of his truck. "Damn!" he hollered at the surprise. He looked out the passenger window and saw a Mexican high tailing it to the brush. Out his window, and now behind him, he saw four border patrolmen and two dogs in hot pursuit. The Border Patrol checkpoint was in the northbound lane of Highway 77 and evidently Poncho's story did not pan out.

Mack was back in the present now and was glad the cut off in Raymondville was just down the road. Now the dark thoughts were replaced by thoughts of fishing and hanging out with his old friend Cody. Finally, he reached the exit he had been looking for so long. He hung a left there and in thirty miles was in Port Mansfield. As he passed the string of signs advertising fishing guides, boat charters and the one café in town, he was glad to see nothing had changed. He buzzed past the RV park and saw it was only half full. At the Pelican bar he took a right and was soon welcomed to the comforting sight of the harbor. The boats were bobbing in their slips. The gulls were flying and squawking. The air was salty and suddenly the world was a better place. He had the windows down and was soaking it all in as he made his way around the harbor to the boat ramp. Happy at his good fortune he saw his friend Cody in his boat that was hitched to his old Chevy truck. He must have just come in; he was in the parking lot organizing the boat. Mack parked his truck and gladly got out to stretch. Cody was absorbed in his task and was easy to sneak up on. In a loud tourist voice he asked, "What does a fella have to do to catch a fish around here?"

Cody slowly stood up to address the idiot that was yelling at him. He turned and saw it was Mack and said, "Well, slap me nekkid! Mack, what are you doing here?"

"I figured I needed to catch some fish and soak my ass in saltwater for a while."

"Well get your ass in that truck and back me in. I just left them biting out on the east flat!"

He quickly backed the trailer and dropped the boat back in the water. He parked the truck and ran back and jumped in the boat. Cody punched it into gear and announced, "We are gonna need some beer." He guided the boat over to the dock at Harbor Bait Store. Mack secured the line and went in to get the beer and ice. He noticed a new girl was working the counter, prettier than usual.

Mack dumped the beer and ice in the Yeti cooler as Cody idled out of the harbor. At the mouth of the harbor Cody yelled, "Coming up!" Mack sat down and instinctively turned his cap around so it wouldn't blow off. The Suzuki 150 roared to life and they were flying across the Laguna Madre.

When the boat was about a mile or so from the harbor Cody shut it down and said, "The trout were in here when I left, maybe they are still at home." He handed Mack a rod and reel with a soft plastic swim bait on it and said, "Let's just see."

The fish were at home. In no time there was a two man limit of ten big speckled trout in the fish box. The action was so fast and furious the two men didn't even have time or inclination to talk other than to trash talk each other's fish. When they hit their limit Cody suggested, "I've been scouting a redfish hole over at Butcher's Island. Let's go look at it."

Cody Delmere was a professional fishing guide and tournament fisherman. After a successful career in the fire service and a messy divorce he decided to forsake life in north Texas and move to the coast. For a man comfortable with himself and who liked to fish, Port Mansfield was the logical place to circle his wagons. The two had met during the big firefighters fishing trip that happened every October. They had been fishing together and had grown to be good friends. Mack was one of the few that could keep up with Cody on his mile after mile marathon wades.

On the way to Butcher's Island Mack was curious about Cody's new boat, "When did you get this boat? I've never heard of a Tiburon boat before."

Asking Cody about anything guaranteed a unique story, "It's a brand new company out of Corpus. Jeff is the owner and he is some kind of hotshot engineer and he likes to fish. He wanted to be able to get back into the real skinny water so he designed this hull. He built the first one in his garage out of plywood. It worked so well that he started building them commercially in fiberglass. I met him at a tournament and he asked me to be on his pro staff, I could use the boat for free for a year if I got on his team. Nice boat, huh?"

Yep, thought Mack, *I knew there would be an interesting story behind this boat.* The boat easily ran through the choppy water. "Yeah, man, most boats would be knocking your teeth loose in this sort of water."

Cody added, "Yeah, it's smooth and dry. It'll run in two inches of water, too."

Mack laughed and called, "Bullshit."

Cody took a posture and said, "Oh, yeah? Hold my beer and watch this." He eased the Tiburon over to the sandy shoreline. He got closer and closer till Mack was bracing himself for the impending sudden stop from running aground. They just kept going though, he could have stepped out of the boat and onto the sand they were so close. Cody ran it out to deeper water and took back his beer. Then he said, "I didn't believe it either. It's got a tunnel hull that funnels water to the prop. The prop is actually above the bottom of the boat when you are running like that. It's a good boat for the skinny water down here." His head snapped around and he said, "Dang, I passed the spot."

He swung the boat around in a wide arc back to the spot, killed the motor and coasted into position. He recommended gold spoons as the lure of choice. They drifted along a weedy shoreline for 200 yards. In that drift they picked up five good redfish. Cody marked a waypoint on his GPS and said, "This will be a money maker come tournament time." Toward the end of the drift Cody brought up the Fire Department.

"So, how's it going at the fire station?"

Mack stared at the passing shoreline for a minute. He knew this was the opening to "The Talk" and right there in this place with his veteran firefighter friend he was ready to talk.

He turned and looked at Cody and said, "It's bad."

CHAPTER 13

Open Wounds in Saltwater

Cody had given 35 years to the fire service. He had an idea of what was coming. He knew how it had to go down. He waited quietly as the boat continued to drift.

Mack started "We had a fire." He cleared his throat. "A little two-bedroom frame house on the edge of town. I know the old man that lived there; he was in the hospital in Fort Worth so I knew it was vacant. A thunderstorm was blowing through so we figured it was a lightning strike. We could see a little fire from the road so my driver caught a plug on the way in. Eric

Watson was my rookie. I think you met him on the trip last year."

Cody nodded his head and said, "Yeah, nice kid."

"We got up to the house and while Eric was getting the hose off I did a 360 of the house. It was dark and raining. I found some fire on the southeast corner coming out a window and the soffit on the roof edge. I couldn't really see what the rest of the windows looked like but I couldn't see any fire in the other rooms. It looked like your average house fire. I came around the corner of the house and Eric had the hose flaked out and was ready to go in. I heard on the radio the ladder truck check on scene and I could see their lights on the road. I figured as soon as they pull up we would go in and put out the fire."

He paused to get a dip of snuff.

"Eric was like a dog on a chain. He wanted in there. I was backing him up on the line. He had the nozzle so he kicked the door to go in. That's all I remember till I woke up in the front yard. I was holding Eric's helmet on my chest and the whole damn house was on fire. All the guys were helping Eric. He got hit pretty bad."

Mack paused to get a grip on himself, he could feel his eyes starting to water.

"Evidently that fire had been burning a while. They said when he kicked that door the air got to it and caused a backdraft explosion, fire came out of every window on that house. They said it blew us 30 feet out into the yard. The explosion blew off his helmet and air mask. I guess that is how I ended up with his helmet.

Mack paused to wipe his eyes.

"He was in front and he shielded me from that blast. He had third degree burns on his face and neck, respiratory burns and some broken bones. He died that night."

There was only the sound of the waves slapping the boat as the boat drifted and the two friends looked at each other, tears welling in Mack's eyes.

"Cody, I know how to read smoke. I know to stay low and go. I know to stand to the side opening a door. I didn't see it that night. It was just a simple fire."

Cody thought a minute then said, "Mack, you are a good fire officer and you are a good firefighter. Sometimes things just go bad. It sounds like you couldn't see what you needed to see that night. I would have handled it the same way. You can't beat yourself up over it. It sounds callous but you just have to let it go."

He knew that was easier said than done. He did feel better though, having told the story to someone he knew and trusted.

Cody asked, "So, is that how you got some time off to come fishing? Are you on injury leave?"

Exasperated Mack replied, "No, I wasn't hurt too bad. Only a concussion. This new young Chief we have put me on indefinite suspension."

Cody exclaimed, "What the hell? For that fire?"

"No, because it was a fatality fire he ordered me to go to a psychiatrist. He had just got back from a seminar on PTSD, post traumatic stress disorder. I refused. I knew I could handle it the way we handle it. He ordered my men not to discuss it with me. He suspended me in his words, "To give me time to think about his offer."

Cody was disgusted, "That arrogant son of a bitch."

"I figured since I had the time I would come down here and try to get my head back right."

Cody agreed, "Saltwater is good for a man." Cody knew the psychological boil had been lanced but he didn't want to squeeze it. He changed the subject when he reached in the Yeti for another beer and said, "Well, we only have two beers left for the ride to the harbor and we almost drifted there anyway, so let's go clean fish."

"Awrighty, thanks for listening, brother." He was grateful for Cody listening to the part of the problem that dealt with the fire department and he felt better for that. He still had a burden, though, that may never come to light. In his deepest and darkest recesses, he still carried the story of Sarah and Little Jake. He was unsure he could ever speak to that.

"It's what we do, brother." And he fired up the big motor.

Upholding the tradition of their group when they got to the harbor, they cracked open the harbor beers and idled to the fish cleaning table.

As they made their way past the boats moored in the harbor, they came to a beautiful 52-foot Viking sport yacht. It stood out from the rest. There was a girl in a bikini oiling the teak wood on the back deck. The girl took second place to the amazing boat. It was 52 feet of sleek white beauty that towered above the water. The teak back deck had a fighting chair mounted in the middle. On the stern was the boats name. BRIGGER. Then in small letters underneath was "IS BETTER".

Mack remarked as they passed, "Damn! Who runs that boat? It's beautiful."

Cody muttered, "Aw, it belongs to some rich fat bastard that comes into port every so often. Way too often. He is a buffoon and nobody in town likes him. The guides hate him. His name is Brigham Johnson.

As they approached the cleaning station, Cody spoke to Mack, "Well, speak of the devil. There's the fat bastard now." Standing at the cleaning table was a tired looking fishing guide cleaning a few fish. Next to him stood a large man with his arms crossed over his belly. He was fully outfitted in the best Columbia fishing clothes available and he was loudly berating the fishing guide about his poor performance securing the day's meager catch. Cody didn't want to do it to the fishing guide but he really wanted to piss off the fat man so he docked his boat and laid two full stringers on the dock. The exhibition locked up the fat man; he was speechless as he stared at the fish.

CHAPTER 14

Sarah's Story

The two friends had a great night catching up with each other over a dinner of fresh fried speckled trout and hush puppies. They did their best to deplete Cody's beer supply. A campfire was built because it seemed like the thing to do and it would keep the mosquitos away. Both men were more comfortable sitting outside than being in the house. When the stories, the laughter and the fire had died down and it got to the time when a man just stares into the coals Mack said, "Cody, I am about whipped. I'm gonna have to hit the hay."

Cody said, "Well I sure am glad to hear you say that. I didn't want to be the first one down but I was sinking fast. That other bed in there is ready for you; if you need anything, just holler. Let's pack it in." The two beer drinkers performed the "Peeing on the Fire" ceremony to put it out and went in the house.

Mack crashed in the bed feeling pretty good. He was sure glad he came down to see Cody and that there were still good times to be had in Port Mansfield. But as he lay there absorbed in thought he began to think of Sarah, the dark thoughts began to rise to the top of his mind. He had no place to go to get away from it so he faced his demon and mulled it over in his mind. To beat the demon you have to look it square in the eye. He could beat it here in this place with his friend. He knew now that was the purpose of his trip.

When Mack was younger and before he settled into the fire service he lived the life of a rodeo cowboy. He was wild and had no ties on him. Until he met Sarah. When he first saw her it was if he had always loved her. He had to convince her to love him back; she didn't trust men, especially cowboys. Her son's father was a cowboy. He left. Little Jake meant all the world to Sarah and she thought she didn't need anybody else, especially a cowboy. Mack quit the rodeo and went to work for a saddle maker in order to show her he could settle down. He courted her in the old fashion sense and was surprised to find he also enjoyed the company of Little Jake. She noticed this. He finally convinced her he was a good man worthy of her attention. The couple was making plans.

Sarah was an attractive woman that caught the interest of men. Hiram Woolsey had an unhealthy interest in her. He was a horse trader and a drunk. He had been bothering her for a while and she had a restraining order on him. He didn't pay much attention to it. When Mack came into the picture there were many violent confrontations between the two men. Mack had easily whipped the old slob many times. Sometimes beating him so badly Sarah had to grab him to make him stop. One night Mack caught him peeping in a window and as he ran back into the cover of darkness Mack fired three shots from his six-shooter at him. That event seemed to settle things down for a day or so.

Mack was headed to Sarah's place one evening after work and he could see a plume of smoke coming from her direction. He thought the man next door had finally lit off that big brush pile. Smoke was not uncommon in the country. When he got to the drive to Sarah's mobile home he could see the smoke was coming from the fire that surrounded her home. It was burning under the trailer and running up the sides. He called the Fire Department and raced to the door yelling her name. Inside he could hear her and Little Jake screaming that scream of primal fear. The scream that only fire can make come from a person. He tried to get in the front door but was driven back by the flames. He tried all the windows and the other door but just couldn't get past the fire. The screams from inside the home pushed him through the pain of his burns. As flames began to shoot out of the windows the screams stopped. Mack stopped too. As far as he was concerned his life stopped. When the Fire Department arrived they found a mobile home fully involved in fire and a sobbing hull of a man bleeding in the front yard, his hair and most of his clothes burned off.

When the Sheriff went to ask his number one suspect, Hiram Woolsey, about the fire, his knock on the door was returned with a gunshot through the door that knocked his hat off. The Sheriff took cover behind an old rusted out horse trailer and Hiram came out of his shack at the horse lot with guns blazing. The old Sheriff calmly placed six bullets in Hiram's chest, all within an inch of the third button on his greasy shirt. Argument over.

The biggest regret in his life, the one that haunted him in his soul, was the fact that he wasn't the one to pull the trigger.

CHAPTER 15

A Chance Meeting of the Unknown

The next morning, the fish left over from fresh fish tacos the night before made some great fish and scrambled egg burritos. Cody ate quickly and was off to start the day. He had an appointment with a woman coming down from San Antonio for boating lessons. She had recently taken possession of her now ex-husbands 32-foot Fountain center console boat. The one he took the strippers out on. She had been told a woman who could handle a boat was super sexy. She was out to increase her marketability.

Cody told Mack to take the Tiburon and go find some fish. He explained his waypoints on the GPS and guaranteed his success. He went on to explain his student had a very nice boat and was a very vengeful woman; so don't expect him back tonight.

As Mack was idling through the harbor he could see the Big Viking boat up ahead. As he got closer he could see a woman sunning on the foredeck. Topless. In Port Mansfield this was as rare as a black man at a clan meeting. So, engaged in the moment, he slowed down. As he came alongside the *Brigger* he saw Brigham Johnson. Brigham saw Mack and yelled, "Hey, come here!"

Mack cut his motor and grabbed the rope Brigham had dropped.

The fat man asked, "Are you a fishing guide?"

"No, sir."

"I recognize you and your boat. You got full limits yesterday and I paid that knucklehead seven hundred dollars for three fish."

"We were one fish short of the limit but, yeah, I saw that."

"What would you charge to take me fishing?"

"I'm not a guide."

"That wasn't the question. What would you charge?"

"Like I said, I'm not a guide."

"Okay, dumb ass, I'll spell it out. If you can get me a limit of trout and redfish, I'll pay you $1000 with a bonus of $100 for each flounder."

Mack thought about it just long enough to form the words, "Get in the boat."

He took the Tiburon to the stern of the *Brigger* and the fat man came out the fish door, clumsily boarding Mack's boat. He shook Mack's hand and said, "I'm Brigham Johnson. You can call me Brig."

"I'm Mack."

They idled to the mouth of the harbor as Brig tried to wedge his generous backside into the racing seat of the Tiburon. When they passed the no wake sign Mack said, "Coming up," and put the gas to it. Brig's hat blew off so they had to turn around and get it out of the water. Mack instructed him, "When I say coming up it means to get ready for wind and speed."

Brig huffed, "You don't have to tell me that."

They roared away across the bay. Since it was a nice morning he figured the topwater bite might be on, he headed to a spot he knew of on the King Ranch shoreline. As he cut the motor and coasted into position he handed Brig a rod with a topwater bait on it. Brig said, "What is this? Where are the shrimp?"

Mack explained, "We are fishing artificials today. You do it like this." He cast the bait out and worked it back to the boat. The fish gods must have been watching; a 24-inch fat trout inhaled the bait in a watery explosion. Mack fought it back to the boat and netted it. "It's sort of like that." Brig was admiring the big fish when Mack held it over the side of the boat and dropped it in the water.

"What the hell did you do that for, you idiot? That was a good fish!"

"We are working on *your* limit." Looking at him with cold eyes he added, "Don't call me an idiot again."

Brig slowly got the hang of it and by the time they got up to the Oak Mott he had a limit of nice trout, despite many misses and reel backlashes. He even caught a bonus flounder on a soft plastic by some submerged cattle pens. Mack was sure glad the bite was on. Now for the redfish. Brig was pretty pumped with his success and was already bragging about his new-found skill.

Mack was hoping to maintain this momentum. He knew Cody wouldn't like it if he used the Butchers Island spot. But like he said, this hole will be a money-maker. He punched in the waypoint on the GPS and said, "Coming up." Brig quickly sat down and turned his cap around. They glided up to the shoreline from yesterday and Mack could see they were still there. The big reds were pushing water and busting bait everywhere.

He explained how to use a gold spoon and Brig went to work. Despite many misses, many spooked fish, three losses and many backlashes, Brig had his limit of three redfish in about fifty minutes. When the last red was in the fish box, Mack said, "Okay, let's go back."

Brig protested, "Hell no, we are staying. This is my best fishing ever!"

Mack reminded him, "The deal was a limit of reds and trout with maybe a flounder. We did that. Coming up." Brig fell into his seat and twisted his cap as the *Tiburon* flew back to the harbor.

When they got back to the harbor, Brig was still griping, to deaf ears, about leaving fish but was also congratulating himself on his great luck and skill. As quickly as he could, Mack took his boat to the stern of the *Brigger* and off-loaded his client. He even helped Brig get his big jelly ass back up through the fish door. Because he knew it would be an exercise in futility to have him clean the catch, he said he would fillet them and bring them back.

Brig said, "Keep them. I'll be back with your money." He returned with eleven $100 bills and Becky, his topless trophy. He was slow to hand over the money. He tried to make small talk while Becky jiggled around. He wanted Mack to see he had the money and what money could buy.

CHAPTER 16

Pirates on the Island

Mack walked out of Cody's extra bedroom and started digging around for coffee makings. He was still a little foggy after a late night at the Pelican Bar. A pot of black coffee would cut the fuzz and bring him into a new day and a new mission. A gnarly old guy at the bar told him he was a shark hunter and the sharks were in heavy at the jetties. The old fisherman had just returned from a week of camping on the beach at the south jetty. The sharks were plentiful and the bull redfish were hitting as well. The whole thing sounded pretty appealing to Mack, to be alone on the beach and catch some monster fish too. He had to figure out the logistics.

Cody came ambling in and the first thing he said was, "Mack, that is one angry woman! I'm not above being a pawn in her game. And let me tell ya, she showed her ex a thing or two last night, whether he knows it or not." After getting a cup of the fresh coffee he added, "She has a nice boat, too. Did you catch any fish?"

"I didn't catch any fish but I caught 1100 dollars."

"In Port Mansfield? That's a week's wages. How'd you do that?"

He went on to tell Cody how he was headed fishing when the opportunity arose and how it all went down.

Cody was impressed, "Dang, you couldn't turn that down."

"Nope, it worked out well, but he is a loudmouth son of a bitch."

"Well, I guess you earned your money. What you gonna do now?"

"I was talking to a guy at the Pelican last night and he said he was doing some good catching sharks at the south jetty. I was thinking about that. What do you think? How is the best way to go about that?" Mack figured Cody was feeling generous given his present mood.

"You either have to drive up the beach from South Padre or go by boat. Driving the beach is an ass whipping. I could run you out there today but the best fishing is at night and I have a charter tomorrow."

"Well, buddy, would it be too much trouble to run me out there today and come get me tomorrow after your charter?"

"Spend the night out there by yourself? There's ghosts of pirates out there man. Weird things happen at night."

Mack huffed, "Huh." Then he added, "I'll bring mine and we will have a party." In his heart he wanted his ghosts to stay on land and just let him fish in peace.

Cody was apprehensive about the plan but helped Mack gather up the camping stuff. They loaded the gear, food and water into the Tiburon. Heavy tackle was needed for sharks and a kayak, to paddle the baits out, was lashed to the side of the boat. As they were getting into the truck to go to the ramp Cody reminded Mack, "You know you are on your own out there don't you?"

"Yep, that's what I'm aiming for."

Reluctantly Cody said, "Well, okay, but take this marine walkie-talkie. It ain't much but maybe you can get a fisherman on channel 16 if you get in a tight spot."

The loaded Tiburon was put in the water and they were on their way. They could hear music getting louder as they proceeded out of the harbor. As they approached the *Brigger,* Kenny Chesney music was banging out of the speakers at an annoying level. Brig and another man were on the back deck with three Mexican girls. It looked like they had started drinking early or hadn't quit yet. When Brig saw the Tiburon he hollered, "Hey, fish masters!" He turned and said something to the girls; simultaneously they pulled up their bikini tops and flashed some boobs. The pair of fishermen just smiled and waved.

Cody said, "Well, that annoying bastard will at least share a little." And as they got to the mouth of the harbor, "Coming up!" They shot down the east cut nineteen miles to the jetties and the Gulf of Mexico.

Cody beached the boat in the sand behind the T head, a line of rocks at the jetty designed to break the waves. He told Mack, "Let's put as much as we can in the kayak and drag it over the sand dune."

With a lot of huffing and puffing they got all the equipment over to the beach side. Cody caught his breath and said, "My charter is an early half day tomorrow so I can probably be back out here around two. Good luck with it and if you have an emergency get on the walkie-talkie, not sure if it will do any good though." As he was walking back over the dune he stopped and said, "If you see the ghost of Jean Lafitte, tell him I said hello."

"Awright, brother, thanks for the ride and I'll see you tomorrow."

Mack busied himself with setting up camp. Every once in a while he could see the top of a big boat passing by the big rock jetty and out to sea. He heard Bob Marley singing "Redemption Song" and thought surely not, but there was the *Brigger* passing by at full volume. When she passed the jetty and got out to sea he could see Brig piloting the boat and the three Mexican girls dancing naked on the back deck. When he couldn't see them anymore he went back to work putting together the shark rigs for the evening fishing. As he worked, he thought of Samantha standing in his window in the early morning light. He was absorbed in that thought and his work so he didn't hear the two Mexicans walk up behind him.

"Heh, señor."

Surprised, Mack spun around to see two Mexican men who had obviously been walking a long time. They each held a gallon jug of water in one hand and an onion sack for a travel bag in the other.

"Whoa, ya'll scared me. What can I do for you?"

The one that spoke English had long greasy hair and a tattoo on his neck. When he smiled he showed a shiny gold front tooth. He asked, "Can you take us across the channel in your little boat?"

Mack looked at the out going tide that was basically a fast moving river and said, "No, man, it's an outgoing tide and we would never make it across."

"But please, señor. We have been walking a very long way and we cannot swim."

"Sorry, guys, it ain't gonna happen."

Long hair said something in Spanish to his gotch-eyed little buddy. He had the sort of eyes that you didn't know which one to look at when you were talking to him. He snickered. Both dropped their onion sacks and pulled out Bowie knives, those cheap gaudy ones you see for sale in the border towns.

Long hair said, "Well then, señor, we will have to take your little boat and your food too."

Gotch eye laughed as he looked in Mack's direction and waved his knife around.

When the knives came out, Mack tensed up but held his ground. He thought, *Well crap. What am I going to do about this?* He was in crisis mode when he said, "Looks like I can't argue with that. Can I get my fishing stuff out of it?"

"Sî, señor."

Mack bent down with his back to the men to get his gear. The two bandits moved in closer. Gotch-eye was rummaging through the groceries. He messed with his tackle till he figured the geometry of his attack was correct. Mack had his heavy redfish rod in one hand, tied on the end was a topwater bait with two oversize treble hooks. In his other hand, he had the kayak paddle. Timing was everything.

Now! Mack spun as he stood and whipped the top-water lure deep into long hair's neck. The surprised bandit dropped his knife, screaming and staggering back. He instinctively grabbed at the object impaled in his neck and sunk the second set of hooks deep into his hand. Gotch-eye stood up from the groceries just in time to catch the blade of the kayak paddle across the bridge of his nose. It laid him open nicely. They were both staggered screaming and jabbering in Spanish. He didn't speak much Spanish, but Mack figured they were saying something to the effect of, "That really hurts!"

He grabbed the knives on the sand and cut long hair loose from his fishing rod then threw the knives into the surf. In an adrenaline fueled voice he said, "Ya'll need to get on out of here now! Vamanos!"

Still screaming Spanish ninety miles an hour, long hair used his free hand to guide the blood blinded gotch-eye back down the beach. Mack hollered at them, "Don't forget your water!" Long hair shot him the finger with his remaining hand.

When he had calmed down, Mack decided he needed to not stay in the area. He knew the tide would slow down soon and he could paddle across, away from retaliation. He hid the ice chest and camping gear in the dunes, it could be picked up later. He strapped the fishing gear to the kayak and pushed off.

Once he passed the calm eddy by the shore he got into the full current. He had misjudged its pull and was doing everything he could to not be taken out to sea. He had his sights set on the opposite shore and was pulling hard on the paddle. His concentration was interrupted by a horn blast. He looked to his right and all he could see was the huge white bow of a very large boat. As the boat shut down, it pushed a large wave of water ahead of it. The escape angle of the kayak was just right to surf the wave to the shore.

The furious captain of the boat was calling Mack every name in the book. Mack was just glad to be alive, sticks and stones, blah-blah-blah. Mack stepped off the kayak and turned to face the assault. The scream-ing orator was Brig. When he saw it was Mack, he hol-lered, "Mack, is that you?"

Mack said, "Yeah, Brig. Could you give me a ride back?"

After they had pulled the kayak on board the *Brigger* and were back underway, Mack told the story of his Mexican encounter. The Mexican girls were in awe of this good-looking gringo fighter, especially since he wasn't the drunk fat bastard they had been with all day. When he was finished with his story, a large man with a mean look in his eye came up from below deck. He was wearing a wife beater undershirt and boxers. He said, "I would have killed them."

Mack looked at him, sizing him up, and extended his hand, "I don't think we have met."

Brig said, "Mack, meet Guido, my personal assistant."

The two men shook hands like two vice grip pliers locked together. Guido said, "You should have killed them." And went back below.

Brig offered, "Guido isn't much on pleasantries but he is very effective." Mack could see the girls were scared of Guido and Mack had an instant dislike for him.

Brig said, "Mack, that was an interesting story. I don't meet many guys like you. You are a tough son of a bitch. We had to come in for fuel, then I was going to take the girls back to Port Isabel. You want to go? We can drop off your stuff and get fuel. We can be back late morning tomorrow unless we get a better offer."

Mack figured free beer, pretty girls and a boat ride would make it easier to tolerate Brig. Cody was going to be busy and he hadn't seen Port Isabel in a while so he said, "Sure, why not."

He forgot to factor in Guido.

CHAPTER 17

What?

As the *Brigger* cruised south down the Intercoastal Waterway to Port Isabel, the two older girls were steadily drugging and drinking. They each took a go at Mack but he turned them down. It became apparent as to why they were staying high. From below, Guido would call for one, then the other, sometimes both. Brig was up top, piloting the boat and he would also call up a girl. The whole thing disgusted Mack; he'd never seen this sort of situation before. He thought to himself, *If I knew it was going to be like this I wouldn't have come.* He tried to stay as comfortable as he could just sitting in the fighting chair, drinking a beer.

The younger girl sat in the corner of the stern looking scared. When both of her friends were below with
Guido, she came to Mack and said, "You look like a
nice man. Can I talk to you?"

Mack sensed something in her voice. "Sure, we can
talk, but I'm not interested in anything else."

"Oh, no no no. I'm not like that. My cousins are
whores and I didn't know it. They put something in
my drink and I ended up on this boat."

"I'm Mack."

"I'm Angie."

"So what's up, Angie?"

"I am afraid that mean man will want me to go
down to the bedroom. I don't want to do that. I want
to be with you; you are a nice man. I saw it."

Knowing this could be a difficult situation, but feeling sorry for Angie and her predicament, he said, "You
are with me."

Angie's face relaxed a little as she said, "Thank
you." Now she looked like an innocent and pretty girl
in her early 20s, one who had no business being on
this boat right now. They talked about her going to
college to be a nurse. He told her he was a paramedic
but told her not to let anyone on the boat know. She
said she was disgusted with her cousins and was going
to tell her **tía** what they'd done to her.

Her cousin staggered back up on deck, high as a kite. After a few minutes, Guido bellowed from below, "Angie, get down here!" She tensed up and fear covered her face. She grabbed Mack's arm. Mack put his hand over hers and said, "You're with me; it's all right."

"Angie!" Guido sounded menacingly close and mean drunk. Angie tried to melt herself into Mack.

Guido stumbled up the steps to the deck and drunkenly yelled, "Angie, get your sweet ass down here! Now!"

Mack didn't get up, he turned his head and said, "She's talking to me."

Guido took a step and Mack got out of the fighting chair. He squarely faced the big mean-looking drunk. Angie shivered behind him. He looked Guido straight in the eye and said, "She'll be down when we are finished talking."

Brig was enjoying the scene from above. When Guido took a step forward he commanded, "Guido, go take a nap!"

He looked up and said, "Yeah, boss." Like a called off dog, he slunk back below.

Mack smiled at Angie and said, "We got a lot to talk about, don't we?" She got her nice face back and they continued on about college, what she liked to do, her whore cousins, how she hated boats now and would probably never drink again.

When the *Brigger* was docked in Port Isabel, Angie touched Mack on the shoulder saying, "Thank you." She jumped up on the dock and was out of there like she was shot out of a cannon. The two whore cousins hung around to be paid. They took Angie's share, saying they would get it to her.

Mack and Brig secured the lines holding the boat and got it back in shape. Guido napped below. Brig commented, "You act like you know your way around a boat."

"I've been on a few."

"You know as drunk as Guido was, he would have beat you to death over that girl."

"He wouldn't have got that far." Then wanting to change the subject Mack said, "You sure have a mighty fine boat here."

Brig stared at him trying to figure him out, then shook his head. "I have had a few, all fine boats. This one is my baby. It took me a while but I finally got to a point I could have the Viking Yacht Company build it to my specifications. She ran me a few million. It may not catch more fish than other boats but I sure look good doing it. You know, appearance is everything. Come below and look at the engine room."

He opened a hatch and they went into the engine room. It was spotless. The twin Detroit diesels purred perfectly. The oversize generator hummed along, guaranteeing plenty of light and air conditioning. There were even A/C vents on the deck. Bulk headed off from the engine room were two propane tanks plumbed to supply fuel for the BBQ grill on deck and the stove in the galley. Back in the tool area there was a workbench lined with perfectly placed tools. For a mechanically oriented man this engine room was a work of art.

Brig proudly asked, "Have you ever seen anything like it?"

"I can't say as I have. It's beautiful."

"Come up top," Brig invited. They climbed back onto the deck. Brig went to the large live bait tank and opened the door underneath; it held two oxygen tanks. Brig boasted, "The bait well is filtered, chilled and oxygenated. I can take bait all the way to Cancun if I want to." He climbed the ladder to the helm and called Mack up, "Come up here and check this out!" At the helm he could control the entire boat. It looked like a control panel from the space shuttle. There was a radar screen, a bottom graph and fish finder and a GPS with auto pilot function. He bragged, "I can set coordinates and punch this button and the boat drives itself." While he was bragging on all of his technology his phone rang. He looked at the caller ID and said, "Oh, man, I have to take this."

Mack climbed down to the deck for another beer. Brig was loud on the phone because he was loud everywhere. Mack couldn't help but overhear.

"Yeah."

"He did? Hot damn!"

"Yeah?"

"When will they probate the will?"

"Okay."

"Yeah, if they are all there, signatures won't be a problem."

"Sure, I can have equipment there in three weeks."

"Okay, yeah."

"Great! Then we are ready to rock and roll, Bubba!"

Mack perked his ear. *Bubba?*

Brig clicked the off the phone, climbed down the ladder and cracked a beer. He seemed to be in the mood to celebrate. "Sometimes, the phone rings and you make money!"

Mack asked, "Good news?"

"Yeah, a big job I've been waiting on just had some roadblocks cleared out of the way. Looks like I won't be on my boat for a while, but it will be worth it."

"Just what sort of business are you in, Brig?"

Brigham Johnson seemed to swell up in front of Mack. "I am in the land development business but in the last few years I have become the best damn golf course builder in the southwest."

CHAPTER 18

Pieces of the Puzzle

Mack wanted to get back to Port Mansfield and do some phone calling. He felt like a jigsaw puzzle had just been dumped on the table in his mind. He had started missing Sam a lot and it would be good to hear her voice and catch up on what was going on at home.

To Mack's relief Brig declared, "We have enough light to get back, let's take her back to Mansfield."

He eased the *Brigger* into the Intracoastal Waterway and they were headed north. Along the Intracoastal on the Texas coast there are small houses built on pilings along the edge of the deeper water. They are used by fishermen as a base of operations on fishing trips in the far reaches of the bay. Brig commented on how cool it would be to have one for a base of operations for fishing trips and parties. He said "I bet those girls from Port Isabel would just love to come out here and lay around on the deck and even if they didn't it's too far to swim back. Who do you talk to about buying one of these houses?"

Mack told him, "They are all privately owned but are built on a lease from the General Land Office of Texas. Those leases aren't granted anymore, so they are like gold. Most are passed down through families, I've never seen one for sale."

"How are they identified?"

"By those official looking numbers on the buildings."

"You take those numbers and find out who owns it?"

"Yep."

"Hmm…," pondered Brig.

As they eased along looking at the houses they came to one that had been torn up in a storm but still had a good dock. Brig took the boat out of gear. As they floated to the front of the house, he opened a compartment and took out a camera. He took a few pictures making sure to get the number on the building. He replaced the camera and took out a flare gun.

He accurately fired a flare into the broken front door. He floated and stared until smoke billowed from every hole on the place.

Brig turned and looking Mack straight in the eye said, "Fire can expedite many a business transaction. I'll bet they will be more inclined to sell now. That is a good dock." He kicked the *Brigger* back into gear. As they were getting on plane Brig, without turning his head said, "If you have any complaints on that I will be glad to wake up the director of my complaint department."

The ride back to Port was quick and quiet. When they got back to the dock, Mack helped secure the *Brigger* and get her in shape to go again. He didn't let on to Brig how much this day had disturbed him. Mack could feel his rage building but he knew he had to keep it in check. They got finished with the work and he jumped up on the dock. Mack kept his voice cool, "Brig, thanks for the rescue and the ride in that nice boat. I'll see you later."

Brig waved and said, "Sure thing, you owe me one." And he disappeared below deck.

Mack left the marina and walked the deserted streets to Cody's house. His mind was in a whirl trying to piece together what he had heard and seen. He had to call Sam to get some more puzzle pieces, he had a feeling something was happening in Stephenville. When he got to the house, it was about time for her to quit for the day. He had moved her to the top of his favorites list and she picked up on the second ring.

"Hey, Sam. How's it going?"

She was glad to hear his voice but didn't really sound like it. "Mack, I was going to call you tonight. I've got bad news."

His heart sank but he asked, "What is it?"

"Buster died today."

He was shocked but almost expected to hear it. He forced himself to ask, "What happened?"

Sam told him how Bubba had let her know that Buster's kids had all come together and gone to the rehab center. They told him his house burned to the ground. The kids decided among themselves it would be in his best interest if he went to a rest home. When he got out of rehab they had a room in a retirement home in Stephenville all set to go, he didn't have to worry about anything.

Sam said, "When I heard that, I went right up to Fort Worth to see him."

"How was he?"

Samantha sniffled, "Mack, he looked like a dead man in a living body. He told me he had nothing else to live for; it was all gone. He wasn't going home. The nurses were even worried because he had stopped grabbing them." She cleared her throat and continued, "I told him you and I would figure out something. We would keep him out of the home."

"What did he say?"

"All he said was thanks. You could tell he had given up." She added, "I got the call this morning that he passed in his sleep last night."

Mack told Sam he missed her but couldn't make any small talk. He told her good bye and hung up the phone. Now he had two ghosts from that damn fire. If he could put this puzzle together there would be a reckoning.

CHAPTER 19

The Devil Exposed

Mack got out of bed before the sun. He got a pot of coffee going and thought of his old friend Buster as it brewed. Buster always said he liked his coffee like he liked his women, hot and strong. The fact was, Buster liked any woman slow enough to catch.

Coastal sunrises are like no other, so Mack poured a cup and wandered on down to the docks for the morning performance. He took Cody's camera just in case there was a Kodak moment. At the docks, it was a buzz of activity. The guides were launching their boats for the morning trips. Clients were running around buying the stuff they forgot. Boats were milling around the fuel pump waiting their turn. Sea gulls and pelicans were making their racket while they dove and fought for a breakfast of dead bait the bait sellers were throwing out.

While he was waiting on the sun, he drank his coffee and scrolled through the pictures on Cody's camera. There were the requisite photos of his clients holding stringers of fish, pics of deer around town and pictures of his boating instruction class with Francine, the divorcee. In one particular photo of note, she was on the bow of the Fountain 32 as it raced across the Gulf of Mexico. She had shed her married life and her bikini top. *In proper circumstances, a vengeful woman is to be admired,* Mack thought.

He came to some pics of a tuna trip Cody had been on. The pictures were 12 night shots of a few men holding up big tuna — huge yellow fin tuna and some very large black fin tuna. There were also some daytime pics of the men holding up big Dorado and a small sailfish. *Pretty impressive trip,* he thought.

The sun began to peek over the horizon. He was lost in thought as he beheld the splendor. The sun rose up into the clouds creating oranges, pinks, purples and yellows. The coastal sun said good morning. The activity had calmed at the harbor store, so he walked on over to see if the pretty girl was working. He needed some more coffee and a can of Copenhagen snuff.

He spent a while talking to the girl while he drank his coffee. She enjoyed talking to a good-looking guy with no intentions, as opposed to the fishing clients in their new Columbia fishing clothes flirting with her. Their conversation was interrupted by Bob Seger music getting louder and louder. She looked outside and complained, "I hate that annoying son of a bitch. Why does he have to play his music so loud?"

Mack laughed as he saw the *Brigger* pull up to the fuel pump. "He sure has a nice boat though."

"Yeah, he has asked me to go out on it a dozen times. I wouldn't board that bitch with six shooters in double holsters on a chastity belt."

Mack laughed, imagining having a customer asking for something like that to be made. *Maybe in Austin.* "I'll go ask him to turn down the music."

"Thank you. Want some more coffee?"

Mack walked down to the fuel dock and yelled, "Brig! Can you turn down the music? It bothers the girl!"

"Screw her, I like this song!"

"Well, hell, I can't hear anything either. Turn it down!"

Brig appeared to be taken aback at being talked to that way by a lowly fisherman but he went ahead and turned it down. He sensed some sort of authority with this fisherman; he just couldn't put his finger on what it was.

Mack asked, "Are you going out today?"

"I thought I would go look for some red snapper then maybe run down to South Padre and start a party."

A neon light of opportunity flashed on in Mack's brain. Perhaps a plan.

"My buddy, Cody, just got back this morning from a tuna trip. He said they left them biting. Want to see the pictures?"

"Aw, man, I love tuna! Let's see those pictures. Come aboard."

Luckily the tuna pics were the first to come up on the camera when Mack turned it on. As far as Brig knew they were from last night. Brig excitedly said, "I got to go do that. So, he left them biting? Can you get his coordinates?"

Mack pulled his loop a little tighter. "Yeah, probably. You need a deck hand? I like tuna, too."

Brig replied, "That's a good idea. I'll pay you $1000 if you will go and help me. Guido ain't worth two cents on big fish."

"Great! It'll be an overnighter, so I'll go get some stuff and get his coordinates."

"Hurry up, I will have her fueled and liquored up by the time you get back."

Mack trotted back to the house to get a jacket, a change of clothes and Cody's microcassette recorder. He dictated short stories while he fished sometimes. Cody gave him some coordinates about six or seven hours away that might or might not hold tuna. Right now, tuna was secondary to the plan.

Mack jogged back to the docks and boarded the *Brigger*. Brig had laid in supplies, which included plenty of liquor. *Perfect*. As they idled out of the harbor with Bob Seger back at full blast, he entered the coordinates into the autopilot. When they cleared the no wake zone, he hit the throttles. When they got to the jetties, he hit the button and the boat roared to life going where it was told.

He climbed off the helm and bellowed into the cabin below, "Guido! Fix me a drink!" Still feeling pretty giddy about the greenlight on his project and now the prospect of big yellow fin tuna, Brig was ready to party. Guido appeared from below with two drinks and the party began.

Mack was unfamiliar with autopilot and uncomfortable with no body at the helm. He stayed up on top and reviewed all the switches and controls while the two big men drank on the deck. After a while, Brig waddled back up to the helm. He mistook Mack's apprehension of autopilot for a keen interest in the boat. He gave him a drunken run down of all the screens and switches and what they operated. He was continually bragging about the boat and how much it cost. He said this boat was everything to him, if he wasn't working he was on this boat. He was a little regretful that this big job was going to take so much of his time but it would be no problem to fly down on rain days or when work slowed.

Mack showed him a spot on the GPS that was a boat wreck he knew about, it usually held red snapper. The tuna wouldn't turn on till dark so they had some time to go get the easy pickings. Brig hit some buttons and the big Viking boat turned and headed to the new spot all on its own.

Since Mack was being paid to be the deck hand he went down to rig the rods for snapper fishing. Guido was on deck and he was no help at all. It seemed his job was to sit and scowl. And drink.

By the time the *Brigger* had reached the programed spot and automatically dropped to idle, he had three rods rigged up and ready to fish. Brig dropped anchor and came down off the helm. Mack handed him a rod and said, "Let's get 'em."

He handed a rod to Guido but he just scowled and said, "I don't fish." Mack shrugged his shoulders and dropped his line over the side.

The action was slow but steady. Mack was surprised at how big the snapper were. Brig was ecstatic fighting the big fish and steadily ordering Guido to fix him a drink. Brig hung into something that was not a snapper, it pulled like a mule. He said he must've hooked a submarine. After a forty-five minute battle, a seven-foot blacktip shark wearily rose to the surface. He had never caught a shark this big and he had to have a picture of it. He yelled, "Get that fish door open!"

Mack said, "It's not a good idea to get a shark that big on the boat."

"I have to get a picture of this!"

So, against his better judgment he gaffed the big pelagic, kicked open the fish door and dragged it on deck. It lay writhing on the deck and snapping its jaws at anything that got close. All of the sudden, Guido came to life. He threw down his drink and sprang from his chair. He grabbed a fish bat and went to waylaying on the big fish's head.

Mack was yelling, "Whoa! Whoa! Whoa!" He wanted to release the fish after pictures.

Guido stood and faced Mack with fire in his eyes. He threw down the fish bat and screamed, "What? First you cock block me then you tell me how to handle a fish?" He pushed Mack down on the slick deck. "You got a problem, man?"

Mack did not like being put on the ground. He grabbed the fish bat laying by his hand and as he stood he hit Guido on the side of his left knee. The big man screamed in pain and was going down. Mack stopped his descent with an upper cut right to his chin. He knew he had one shot and had to give it everything he had. The big mean man flew backwards and through the open door to the galley below. He was out of action.

Brig stood aghast at Mack's speed and ferocity. Mack was rubbing his hand and said, "Sorry about that."

Still big eyed, Brig said, "Mighty impressive. I guess I will have to fix my own drinks for a while."

Mack asked him, "Where should we put the shark?"

Brig dismissed it and said, "Aw, throw it over. I just wanted a picture."

Mack was disgusted but he did it.

Brig took a bottle and went back up top to hit the previous coordinates, and they were off again to the tuna spot. Mack used the onboard wash down hose to clean up the carnage. He got the deck back in order to fish. When he got to the door leading below, he looked at the sprawled out Guido to confirm he was breathing. The behemoth was snoring loudly, so Mack closed and locked the door. He thought it odd that Brig would have a door lock on the outside of the door.

Mack was glad for the autopilot. It allowed the boat Captain to get drunker with every glass. The big Viking sport fisher knew what it had to do and as soon as they got to the spot, it dropped to idle. Mack went up top and hit the anchor button, dropping the anchor. Brig focused his eyes and said, "Oh, you were paying attention, huh?" Mack went to work changing the set ups from red snapper to tuna rigs. Brig sat and watched as he worked. When everything was put together and ready to go Mack said, "Let's just wait till it gets right. The sun should be down in an hour or so."

"Well," Brig slurred, "while we are waiting and Guido is taking his nap, I got a question I want to ask you. I ain't never seen anybody put down Guido before. You are a bit of a bad ass. You can handle a boat and can catch fish, too. How would you like to come to work for me?"

Mack got up and freshened Brig's drink then asked, "What would I be doing?"

Brig said, "Handling this boat and stuff."

Mack went over to get a beer from the ice chest and as he bent over he switched on the tape recorder in his pocket. He cracked the beer and said, "The boat I can handle, it's the other stuff I'm wondering about. You talking burning stuff?"

Brig let out a big drunk laugh, "Boy, I like your directness. You don't beat around the bush do you? You talking about that old fish house?

"Since this is a job interview, I was wondering about that comment you made about fire expediting a business transaction. What sort of business you running?"

Brig focused his blurry eyes on Mack and said, "Hell, boy! I am the best damn golf course builder in the world! That's what sort of business I'm running. I just got a big job up in Stephenville to build a golf course at some horse place. It's a big job and I'm gonna get rich. My client has investors just throwing money at the project. We were held up on starting by some old dumb ass cowboy who wouldn't sell the land. Said it was his homestead. Well wouldn't you know it, while the old fart was in the hospital his house burned down! He died in the hospital and I got a call from my man up there telling me his kids were going to sell for less than I offered the old fart. I expedited the business transaction!"

Mack was furious and could barely contain himself. He made sure the fish bat was not in reach. He asked, "So, you burned down his house? Isn't that pretty hard to do without getting caught?" He handed Brig the bottle and enough rope to hang himself.

Brig feigned shock, "Me, burn down a house? That would be illegal. Mother Nature sort of did it. This time of year, they have a lot of thunderstorms up there. I just helped out. I put a lever in a window by the fuse panel with a little bucket on one end and some copper wire on the other. Mother Nature fills that bucket with rainwater and those copper wires raise up and short out the fuse panel. Everywhere a wire touches wood you got fire. Lightening is always with the storm. Bingo! You got you a lightning strike house fire. Fool proof! Anyway as far as an investigation goes, I made the right investment with the right people and the investigator got suspended. He left town and ain't been heard from since! We start work as soon as I take possession of the land."

Mack was looking at the fish bat and the gaff pretty hard. Things were coming together pretty fast now. When he looked at Brig, Mack saw someone from the past — an evil low-life who took everything from him. He had to fight the urge not to allow that kind of hate to control him. The rage he had was boiling over now but he managed to hold it. He knew he had to change the subject. "So, you are starting that real soon. Would I be building golf courses?" he asked as calmly as he could.

Brig tried to stand to get some ice but fell back into his chair. He said, "Golf course building would be a waste of your assets. I got Mexicans for that. You would be my personal assistant in charge of maritime operations with occasional tasks of personnel management. You seem to be enough of a bad ass to do that. I'll probably leave Guido on land. Sometimes my client up there needs some guidance as far as proper business practices go."

Mack said, "Well, thanks for the offer. I will give it some serious consideration. Let's fish." And he shut off the recorder.

Brig was too drunk to cast a rod so Mack had him thinking he was fishing with cut bait. There were no tuna and he was glad. He kept Brig's drink iced and fresh, like a good deck hand should. Till he passed out.

He considered throwing both of the men overboard. *A drunk falling overboard is a plausible story.* His rage told him that would be too easy; they had to hurt more than that.

He went up to the helm and lifted the anchor. The big boat easily fell into gear and was headed back to home port. He sure wanted to be back on land by the time Guido woke up, so he was airing out the boat pretty well in the calm seas. He wanted to hit the post office then discuss plans with Cody and make sure he would go in on it with him. His plan was to have a reckoning for this fat, fire-starting bastard.

CHAPTER 20

Making the Sun Come Up

Mack brought the *Brigger* back to her dock in the early hours of the morning and secured her mooring. He took the catch of red snapper and filleted them, letting them bleed heavily on the deck. He lightly washed it down so it was just pink with some blood here and there. It looked like poorly washed down carnage. He climbed up on the dock and left the two passed out drunks where they lay.

He walked the dark streets back to the house and fell into bed. He slept easily, even though he was anxious to tell Cody what was going to happen. This night he had no dreams of the fire, only dreams of the sea.

He awoke to the smell of coffee and the racket from Cody rummaging around the kitchen. He went into the kitchen and over coffee told Cody what he had learned. He played the tape for him just to be sure it was audible before he sent it off to Sam. Her instructions were to give the tape to a customer of his, a Texas Ranger. No one in town was to be trusted. He ran his plan by Cody for a second opinion. Cody picked up on Mack's resolve and was just a little scared of it, but wholeheartedly agreed with his tactics. He said, "I agree with your plan but it is a pretty ballsy move. You are hitting this guy pretty hard."

"Cody, this guy took all Buster had and it killed him. He took all Eric had and ever will have. He burns things; I cannot let it go. Fire took all I had one time and almost killed me. This is a reckoning, an eye for an eye. I'm taking all he has."

Cody stared at Mack with steely eyes.

Mack told him, "We will need an off shore boat."

"I bet I can borrow Francine's Fountain. I'll probably have to give her a good doing to get it, but I will take one for the team."

Mack laughed and said, "Thank you for your sacrifice, my friend."

He left for the post office and Cody shaved and cleaned up to get working on borrowing the Fountain 32. Mack put the cassette and instructions in the shipping box and overnighted it to Sam in Stephenville. He called her to let her know it was coming, but only got her voicemail. He left a message saying it was coming and to please work quickly on it. He said nothing of his plan but he did say he wouldn't be around a phone until tomorrow morning. After the post office, he went down to the docks to check on Brig. As he approached, he could see the big guy moving around like a man with a hangover.

He walked down the dock to the boat and said, "Good morning. How you doing?"

"Aw, man, I must have had a good time."

Mack smiled and said. "Yeah, we tore up the tuna."

"Where are they?"

"You said throw them back."

"Oh, man! I musta' been really drunk. What did I do that for? I wanted some in the box."

"Well, I tried to keep some but you said no and you're the boss. I tried to clean the boat as best I could in the dark. It was a mess, looks like I missed some. I'll come back and get that."

"Yeah, whenever." Brig scratched his belly and looked around. He made that dry mouth lip smacking sound then he said, "I'm gonna go get something to eat."

"OK, I'll be back to finish the boat after breakfast."

Mack went to the harbor store to kill some time and to talk to the pretty girl. He had to let Brig get well into breakfast. He finished there and went by to see if Cody was back. He was not. Probably still in negotiations for the use of the Fountain 32. He went by the liquor store to get some Everclear, pure alcohol and the jet fuel of alcoholic drinks.

He figured the time was right so he went back to the *Brigger* to start cleaning up. Brig and Guido were still at breakfast, so he was alone on the boat. He ran some water on the deck then went to the liquor cabinet. He emptied the full bottles half out and filled them back with the Everclear. The partial bottles were substantially spiked. He then went to the engine room to refresh his mind on the layout. Back on deck, he checked his surroundings and the coast was clear. He disconnected the oxygen bottles from the live well and took them to the engine room. He secured the hatch and got back on deck just in time to see Brig walking alone down the dock. He looked a little more chipper with some food in his belly. He was a trained professional in hangover maintenance and rallied quickly.

As he boarded, Brig commented, "Man, what a mess. We must have torn them up last night."

"We sure did! The action was fast and furious, just like Cody said it would be. Those dudes bled all over the deck. It looked like the Manson family was fishing. That 90-pounder you caught really bled a lot."

"I caught a 90 pound tuna?"

"You don't remember? You fought him for an hour. I didn't think you were that drunk. I couldn't figure out why you wanted to throw them back, but you were firm on it."

"Hell, I don't know. I guess I *was* drunk. I sure wanted some though. Tuna steak and cold beer will attract a lot of babes on South Padre."

"Well, we could have filled up the boat. They are probably still there; conditions haven't changed. I haven't seen fish like that in ten years."

Brig did a quick physical evaluation and said, "I feel better. You want to go back tonight? I think we ought to. I got to have some tuna, so I'm telling you right now if I say throw them back, don't do it. Put them in the box." Brig looked around like he was getting his bearings and said, "By the way, did you drive my boat back?"

Mack stood up from scrubbing the deck and said, "Yeah. You were passed out and Guido was knocked out. I figured it would be better to get you back in port, being passed out and all."

Brig scowled, "Nobody but me has ever driven this boat."

"I was the only one available at the time."

Brig squinted at him and said, "You got some balls, boy. I wasn't so drunk I don't remember that job offer though, you thought anymore about that?"

Mack shrugged as he worked and said, "Still thinking on it. I don't know if I want to leave down here."

"You might not have to. It might work if you stayed here to maintain the boat and keep fish spotted. You would have to travel some though. At times, there would be meetings with clients and associates where your input would be beneficial. Sort of like that conversation you had with Guido. You scared the hell out of him, boy. He doesn't want to be around you. So, when are we going fishing? I want to hit them while they are hot."

Mack smiled inside and said, "How about leaving around 6:30. That way we could rest today and be there ready to go at dark. They started an hour after sundown."

"That would be great."

Mack stowed the brushes and gave it a final rinse. "There, all ready to mess up again. Oh, by the way, can you pay me from yesterday while I'm here?

Brig said nothing when he pulled out his wallet and handed over ten 100-dollar bills.

Mack stepped up on the dock and said, "I appreciate it. See you at six."

Mack got back to the house and crashed in the bed. Cody woke him up when he came in. "We got a green light on the Fountain. The negotiations took the starch out of me. I'm gonna take a nap."

Mack woke up for the second time around 4 o'clock. He put on clean shorts, a button up shirt and a clean cap and headed to the docks. He could see Brig fidgeting around the boat; he wanted to get going. When he walked up, Brig said, "You sure dress nice to go tuna fishing."

Mack replied, "Man, I am sorry. I can't go. This sweet thing up in Raymondville called me with an offer I couldn't refuse. She is the best-looking girl in town and I can't pass this up. I got some new coordinates that Cody used last night. It's closer in and the fish were just as good." He handed Brig a piece of paper with the numbers on it.

Brig took the paper and was miffed when he said, "You horny little bastard. If you go to work for me this stuff ain't gonna fly! But I can't say as I blame you."

"I am really sorry but it is just too good to pass up. Just use the baits that are on the rods and you will kill 'em. That's what they hit last night."

"Damn, I'm going with you or without you. As soon as my associate gets here, I'm gone. He just called to tell me he had turned off at Raymondville."

"Who do you have coming to visit?"

"Oh just a guy that helped me remove some roadblocks on that big job. He has some time on his hands and we can combine a business meeting with some fishing. He said he needed to leave town for some vacation anyway."

Mack turned and walked away toward the house. He was mad at this unforeseen circumstance and that the plan would be delayed. *Everything is in place and Brig's knucklehead friend has to show up and mess it up. Collateral damage involving innocent bystanders is never a good thing.* He would have to tell Cody the plan was aborted. They might as well just sit and drink beer tonight and come up with plan B. That wasn't a good plan either, because they were out of beer at the house. *Dang it!* So, he turned and headed to the harbor store for a case of beer and some stimu-lating conversation with the pretty girl.

While he was talking to the girl at the counter, he noticed she was speaking and acting differently today, just a little more attentive. He chuckled and thought, *Well I guess clothes do make the man.* Out in the harbor, Aerosmith could be heard drifting over the water. She said, "That bastard is back!"

The *Brigger* pulled in for fuel, and Mack could see three men on the boat, he figured one had to be the "Interrupter." He wore a Hawaiian shirt and a stupid looking hat. As they fueled the boat, he got off and walked up to the store. From a distance, Mack thought it looked sort of like Big Al. As he got closer to the door Mack saw him better. "Damn, I gotta go!" He ran out the front door leaving his beer on the counter.

Game on!

Mack ran back to the house, excited that the plan was back in play. He quickly shed his nice clothes and put on his bathing suit. He woke up Casanova Cody and asked, "You got any swim flippers?"

Cody roused and said, "Yeah, under the TV, I think."

The two conspirators hopped in Cody's truck to drive to Francine's house on the water where the Fountain was docked. They snuck around the side of the house to the dock and jumped in the boat before she noticed. Cody said, "Hurry, I don't want her to see me. If she catches me, we will be here for another hour. That woman has an insatiable appetite for fun." They were in the fast boat and underway quickly. While Cody was driving the boat, Mack entered the coordinates and the GPS automatically plotted their course.

The wind was too loud to talk, so they rode in silence. As the sun closed on the horizon, they got close to the spot. They could see the *Brigger* anchored about a mile away, close to an abandoned oil rig. They took the Fountain to the downwind side and dropped anchor.

On the water, sound carries very well and down-wind even it's better. Cody dropped it to idle, and the twin 300HP 4 strokes just purred. Leaving them running was the prudent thing to do this far out.

Cody asked, "What do we do now?"

"Just wait. Oh, by the way, Big Al is on the boat."

Cody was speechless. His eyes were wide as he looked at Mack then the *Brigger*. He quickly did this six times then just started laughing. He caught his breath and said, "The plot thickens."

When it got dark, they pulled anchor and moved up to where they could hear conversation coming from the big white boat.

Evidently the trio had gotten into the hot bottles early and were well on their way to stupid drunk. Brig was hollering and cussing because he couldn't cast the rod and there weren't any fish to cast to anyway. Big Al was hollering in Spanish and Guido was yelling about how he was going to kick Mack's ass. Soon the oratory became less intelligible, just drunken babble. Mack told Cody, "It won't be long now."

When it had been quiet for 45 minutes, Cody pulled anchor and eased up closer. Mack put on his swim fins and moved to the back of the boat. He slid into the inky black water and swam toward the now silent *Brigger*. When he was away from the boat and void of all security, he realized full well that he was no longer at the top of the food chain. Sharks had taken his place there. He hoped his target boat had caught no fish to lessen the likelihood of sharks. Either way, right now he was the predator.

He went to the stern of the boat and pushed open the fish door. The only sound was that of the generator and the air conditioner. An empty whisky bottle rolled around on the deck. He removed his fins in the water and climbed up on the deck. Looking in the door that led below he could see the three men passed out in various poses. He climbed up to the helm and cut power to the generator; the boat was now dead quiet. Using his flashlight, he went to the hatch for the engine room. He entered and went to the bulkhead door where the propane tanks were. He opened it then disconnected the supply lines on the tanks. He opened the valves on each of them. They spewed the heavier than air gas that fell to the bottom of the boat. He quickly went back to the hatch and before he left, he opened the two oxygen bottles.

When he was back on deck, he could hear sounds from below; it sounded like hogs rooting around. He quickly slid back into the water and put on his swim fins. He didn't know what sort of time he had now, so he swam quickly through the dark back to the Fountain.

He climbed back aboard and told Cody they should move back at least 500 yards. It was hard to gauge in the dark and the *Brigger* now had no lights on it. They guessed it to be about right and Cody idled the boat. He had found some beers and handed one to Mack. He asked, "So what do we do?"

Mack stared in the direction of the *Brigger* and icily said, "Wait for the sun to come up."

It was a warm night and it didn't take long for the galley of the *Brigger* to get uncomfortable enough to wake up a drunk. After about an hour, they could hear a drunk and angry Brig yelling "What the hell? Where is the air conditioning? Wake up you dumbass! It's hot!"

There was lots of cussing and clamoring as they all got out on the back deck where it was cooler. The sounds carried across the water very well. Brig tried to climb to the helm and fell off. More yelling. He got to the helm and the last thing they heard was, "Why is the damn generator turned off?"

Suddenly the beautiful Viking Sportfisher, Brigham Johnson's dream boat and according to him his only respite, erupted with an explosion and a huge ball of fire. The pressure wave was noticeable from 500 yards away.

Cody said, "Well I'll be switched. The sun did come up."

Mack said, "Yep, on a new day."

He Came Back Alone

Samantha and Mack sat on the deck of the rented apartment over the Harbor Bait Store. When he got back to the harbor last night, he had a yearning to be with her. Mack called her and asked if she could fly down if he sent her a ticket. Sam jumped at the chance. She'd never seen the ocean before and Port Mansfield seemed like her kind of place. Mack sure painted a pretty picture of it on the phone.

He picked her up at the Harlingen airport yesterday evening, fed her some of the best Mexican food to be had and took her to a store to get some suitable attire for the south Texas tropics. She hadn't owned a bathing suit till now. The shorty shorts and thin nylon fishing shirt were a long way from Wranglers and pearl snap shirts, but she adapted quickly.

As they sat on the deck and had morning coffee, they could hear the morning news on the TV in the living room. Mack's attention shifted from her thin yellow fishing shirt when he heard the news man say,

"Three men were rescued from an abandoned oil platform late yesterday. The Coast Guard was alerted just after midnight, by an anonymous radio transmission about a boat on fire about fifty miles off the coast. A search was mounted, but the boat in question could not be located in the area. Just before the search was to be called off, the men were spotted clinging to an oil platform. The three were suffering from burns and exposure. Two of the men were wanted by the Texas Rangers for questioning about a fire that killed a firefighter in central Texas a few weeks ago. The third man was the Fire Chief from Stephenville, Texas. This is all the information we have at this time but will be following the story for you."

The two looked at each other with surprise. Mack said, "Well, I'm glad they weren't killed."

Sam asked, "What did you think would happen?"

He thought a minute then said, "I really didn't know. The more I got to know Brig and how he worked the more I hated him. Actually, hate is not a strong enough word. That boat meant everything to him, just like Buster's house meant everything to him. I wanted to take that from him. He also had no remorse for Eric dying in that fire. I guess I was full of rage and really didn't care what the end result was. Brig pretty much said he had bought off Big Al, so I had no concern for him either when he entered the picture."

Mack stood and went to the railing. He stared at the harbor for a minute. Sam watched him, like she did with a bad horse, waiting for him to continue. He took a deep breath and exhaled then spoke of himself, "The guy that went out on the ocean that night did not come back, he stayed out there. I am here now. I am back."

Sam got up and went to him. She wrapped her arms around him and said, "I am glad."

The two lovers held each other as they watched the fishing boats leave for the day. Each soul touched the other as they held their embrace. Both thought it couldn't get any better than this moment right now.

Finally, Mac said, "Why don't I show you the best breakfast burrito this town has to offer? There is a little barbeque place on the main road and they do it up right."

"I could eat. I'll get dressed."

He stopped her, "You are just fine the way you are, shorts and a fishing shirt is the standard down here. Let's run by and see if Cody is around. I'd like you to meet him. I bet he would like to meet you, too."

When they pulled up to Cody's house, he was outside messing with his boat. As they got out of the truck, Cody made a beeline for Sam. He wasn't going to wait for introductions. "You must be Sam; I'm Cody. Sure glad to meet you." He shook Mack's hand, also and said, "Oh, yeah, glad to see you, too." Cody started laughing at the slight and asked, "What do ya'll have going today?"

Mack said, "We were going to go get a burrito. You want to come? Free food."

"Can a fat baby fart? Heck yeah, I want to go." And he headed to the truck.

At the restaurant Sam agreed it was the best burrito she'd ever had. Who would have thought barbeque for breakfast could be so good? While they ate, Sam asked Cody, "So, where is the beach down here? All

I've ever heard about the coast is going to the beach. I don't see one."

Cody said, "It's about 19 miles that way," and he pointed to the east. "All this water you see here is the Laguna Madre; it's all between the mainland and the island. The beach and the ocean are on the other side of Padre Island; you can't see it from here. I was going to do some running around the bay today exploring for new fishing holes. Ya'll want to come? We could run out the east cut and I'll show you the beach."

She was tickled at the thought and said, "I've never been in a boat on the ocean before, I would love it!" Sam was amazed that anyone would just run around on the largest expanse of water she'd ever seen. It was a little intimidating. She was starting to like Cody and his sense of freedom.

Cody laughed and said, "Captain Cody's beach tour is now in operation. The boat leaves as soon as we can get it in the water."

The trio left the barbeque joint to get the boat and get it in the water. Sam was excited to be going to see something she never thought she would. She was hurrying the boys along; she didn't want to wait. They launched the boat off the trailer and went by Harbor Bait to get some snacks and drinks.

When Mack walked in with Sam, the pretty girl at the counter was not nearly attentive to Mack as she had been. Mack noticed this and laughed to himself when he thought, *Oh, this is where that was going.* He'd just thought she was friendly. So he endured her hard stare, paid for the stuff and got back on the boat.

They idled to the mouth of the harbor and Cody said, "Coming up." The Tiburon roared to life and they were off. Mack caught Sam as she almost fell backwards off the leaning post. She was grinning ear to ear.

The boat raced across the huge expanse of water to the east cut. Sam was amazed at the sea birds diving for baitfish all around. She'd never seen a pelican before and loved it as they easily glided along undulating over the water, getting within inches of it. She saw two dolphins breach the water and was like a little kid squealing with delight. Mack was really glad he had brought her down here and that she was loving it so.

They got to a series of islands on both sides of them. Cody explained these were spoil islands, made from the sand that was dredged up to make the deeper channel they were running in now. The channel had to be deeper to accommodate bigger boats that came in from the Gulf of Mexico to Port Mansfield. When they passed one very large island that was white sand dunes; Sam commented that it looked like the sand dunes in a Colorado national park.

When they got to the rock jetties she could see the large breakers rolling in at the mouth of the jetty. She gripped Mack's arm a little tighter and asked, "Are we going through that?" She was getting nervous.

Mack laughed and reassured her, "No, we could but it would be pretty sporty. We will pull in over here."

Cody guided the boat to a calm spot behind the T head and beached the boat. He told the pair, "If ya'll want to do some beach walking, I'll let you out here and be back in an hour or so after I do my running around."

Mack said, "Take your time, bud." He grabbed some water bottles and jumped out of the boat. Sam didn't wait for any help; she jumped out right behind him. The jump splashed some water on her face, she licked her lips and exclaimed, "It really is salty; how cool!"

Cody backed the boat out into the current, turned and headed off. Sam and Mack climbed over the sand and rocks and walked out onto the beach. It was deserted as far as they could see. They were on the other side of the channel from where Mack had met long hair and gotch-eye, so he wasn't concerned with having company.

He told Sam the story of that encounter and she thought it was hilarious that he would send two bandits off the way they came in such a condition. Knowing he could handle himself in a situation like that made her feel safe out on the deserted beach.

Robinson Crusoe and his girl Friday walked north on the beach for a while. She picked up every seashell she saw for the first few hundred yards then she figured out they all pretty much looked the same. She kept saying how deserted and beautiful it was and how she understood now why Mack wanted to come down here to sort things out. She was absorbed in the beauty of it all.

They walked and Mack told her all he knew about the island. How cannibal Indians lived there when the Spanish first landed, about the ghosts that were supposed to be there and about the rumors of treasure buried in the dunes. She loved hearing the stories and told him how far removed it was from her world of the reservation and horse ranches.

They were watching the waves roll in when she asked, "You can swim in the ocean, can't you?"

He said, "Sure, you just have to be careful"

"Dang, I wish I'd brought my bathing suit"

Mack looked one way then the other and said, "I don't see a soul for thirty miles, don't let that stop you."

She giggled and said, "I guess you are right," as she took off her shorts and shirt. He watched her as she walked into the waves breaking on the beach. He committed the sight to memory; he never wanted to forget the way the waves wrapped around her tight, naked body. She turned and waved for him to come in the water, too, and he couldn't argue. They skinny-dipped until their skin began to sting from the sun. He told her they probably ought to get back to the jetty to meet Cody. "No need in spoiling the trip with a full-body sunburn," he said.

She laughed and said, "Yep, most of my parts have never seen the light."

They got dressed and walked hand in hand back to the pick up point. Mack could see Cody's boat in the distance, heading their way.

Cody beached the boat and yelled, "All aboard!" As Sam was climbing back into the boat, Cody noticed her shiny black hair was wet and her dry clothes. He looked at Mack and raised his eyebrows. Mack just winked. Cody chuckled, he was glad for his friend.

Sam noticed and asked Cody, "What are you chuckling about, Cody?"

He replied, "Sometimes, I just think of funny things. Ain't this a great day?"

She said, "It sure is. Thanks for bringing me out here. I have never seen anything like it. I see now why you guys like it so much down here."

"Yep, there sure are a lot of interesting things out here," he said as he backed the boat off the bank and turned to head back.

When they got back to the harbor Cody showed Sam what a harbor beer was, and she enjoyed the tradition. As they idled to the boat ramp he asked, "So, when are ya'll going to head back?"

Mack said, "Sam has to get back to her horses and I guess I ought to get back and see where I'm at on this suspension. I'll make some phone calls today and see if I still have a job. Big Al is probably in a mess now, so things may have changed. I guess we will leave first thing in the morning."

Cody said, "I hate to see you go but I guess you need to get back to reality. The bright light is shining on the bad guys now. I expect there will be some changes."

CHAPTER 22

Coming Back

Mack awakened alone in the bed. He felt incredible. Through the small apartment he could see Sam standing out on the deck, taking in the view. She had really taken a liking to the coast and he was glad. He would be bringing her back here. Not just because it was a great place to be but also because now it was a particular place. It was the place where he had bared his soul to Samantha. Now she knew all of what Mack was about, all his secrets.

Last night as they sat overlooking the water, he started talking and she pulled it out of him. He told her all about Sarah and Little Jake. He cried as only a man can cry with the woman he loves when he told her about the fire. She cried with him while he told her about how the horse was there with him at his lowest point and made him use all his bullets.

She told him when she was little her grandfather spoke of a spirit horse. Sam was amazed when she told Mack that the spirit horse must have been there with him. When they were both cried out and all his cards were on the table, they went to bed. They made love with the passion that only an indescribable emotional bond can create. The sort of love that involved emotions, hearts and souls, not just the physical. Because of that, and because of her, and the fact that his demons had been cast out, Mack felt as if he was a new man. He felt free.

The smell of coffee was absent from the morning though. He chuckled as he got out of bed; she was waiting for him to make it. He didn't mind. After he made a fly by on the deck to tap her on the bottom, he went and got the coffee going. While it was brewing, he went back out and wrapped his arms around her, and she leaned back into him.

She sighed and said, "I have been to a lot of places in my life but this has to be one of the best. Now, after last night, it will always be a special place to me. I am so glad you opened up and told me those things."

"Sam, I never thought I would be able to tell those things to anybody. I tried really hard not to, ever. Not even to myself. That was my deepest secret and I am glad you know it; I can trust you. I feel free from that burden now; I feel like a different man. But, let's never talk about it again. Okay?"

"I understand," she said as she gazed out over the harbor for a while. She broke the silence and changed the subject when she said, "It is so quiet and secluded. It is so cool being on the water here and seeing the deer everywhere is great. I guess they are just really accustomed to seeing people; they are not spooky at all."

Mack agreed. "There are not very many places like it left on the Texas coast, most every place is built up and crowded. People come here to fish and look at deer; that is about it. I bet they would run you out of town if you shot one."

She turned in his arms and looked him in the eyes and asked, "So, I guess we have to go back today?"

He said, "I hate to but I guess we ought to get back. I'm going to make some calls and see what is going on back home. Something is bound to be happening in the Fire Department. We will be back down here though; I can guarantee that."

She made one last big sweep with her eyes and said, "Well, let's drop the reins and head that pony north." She walked back in the room and yelled, "After some of your coffee!"

Mack really did not want to leave this moment.

Eventually, they packed up the pickup and went to see Cody. He must have had a charter because he wasn't at home. As they passed the parking lot at the boat ramp, Cody's truck was there with an empty trailer. Mack told Sam, "Let's go see if he is getting bait and ice at the store, if he's not there he will be gone for the day."

As they pulled up to the store they could see they just missed him. He was idling away with two clients. Mack gave a toot on the horn and Cody turned around. He saw it was Mack and gave a wave and a thumbs-up. He blew Sam a kiss and was off around the bend.

As the couple drove on out of town he told her the story of Cody and how he came to live down here. "A divorce and retirement all in the same year led him to reinvent himself in the solitude of Port Mansfield."

Sam remarked, "Well, he sure seems happy and comfortable here. He is a really nice guy."

Mack agreed, "Yeah, he sure is happy here. He's a good friend, too — the kind you can always count on."

Mack was still thankful for his silent accomplice on his mission.

As they began the long drive north, Sam was interested in the landscape they were driving through. She had never been this far south and was amazed at how flat it was. Mack told her, "Most of the land we're driving through for a while either was or still is the King Ranch." She was familiar with the name because the King Ranch had been breeding some mighty fine horses for a long time. She had never ridden one but always heard how good they were.

She told him on the next trip she wanted to go by the headquarters in Kingsville and see it. She wasn't too much on cattle.

She was impressed when Mack told her that the red cattle they were seeing along the way were the Santa Gertrudis; the breed invented by the King Ranch specifically to survive in the Texas tropics. "The cowboys that work the ranch are called Kinenos. They're mostly Mexican and have done it for generations." She loved the history of it all.

As interesting as it was, the monotony of the endless mesquite brush got boring. Sam laid down in the truck seat with her head in Mack's lap, and soon she was asleep. Mack hit the roadside gravel a few times when he stared at her as she slept.

He decided to use the quiet time to call Jim Bob, the Firefighters Association president. He was curious about what was happening since Big Al got his hand caught in the cookie jar hanging out with bad men. The cell phone rang a few times and Jim Bob picked up.

"Hello, this is Jim Bob"

"Hey, Jim Bob, this is Mack. What's going on back home?"

"Well, speak of the devil. Mack, I'm in the Chief's office right now and we were just talking about you."

"Is the Chief there?"

"Well, the new chief is. Chief Fuentes has been suspended pending an investigation into his recent activities. Assistant Chief Taylor is the interim chief now. We were just talking about your situation and were wondering when you can be back at work."

"No kidding. I will be back in town tonight. What shift is it? I have lost track. I can be back at work when you tell me to be. I'm looking forward to it."

"Chief Taylor says your regular shift is day after tomorrow. How about you report for duty then? Come by the administration building to talk to him some time that day."

"I'll dang sure be there! Tell him thank you for me, Jim Bob. And thank you, too. I'm sure you had a part in it."

"You are sure welcome, my friend, I'll see you at the station."

Mack shook Sam awake and said, "Guess what?"

She sat up and rubbed her face then she said, "Are we home?"

Mack laughed, "Not quite, but when we get there I'm going back to work!"

She hugged him and said, "That's great! What did they say?"

"Big Al got some of his own medicine and got suspended while they investigate him. The interim chief wants me back at work day after tomorrow."

"I figured he might get some dirt on himself, your Texas Ranger friend was just as interested in him as he was Brig when he listened to that tape. I hope they hand his ass to him."

Mack said, "I guess there is a lot of talk going on at the department about all this. Sounds like I will have a lot to catch up on when I get back."

Sam got serious, "How do you feel about going back Mack?"

That sort of knocked the shine off his mood. He thought about it a minute then said, "You know, I'm ready. I feel better. Payback has been made. I am regretful about all that happened with Eric and Buster but it happened. There is no changing that. Let the past be the past. I'm going to put that away and go on living. When I get back to the station, we will put it behind us as a crew. I have dealt with all of it and if my guys need me I can help them with it too. It's gonna be a new day."

The remainder of the trip was spent talking about the future and cussing the traffic in Austin.

They arrived at Samantha's place at the Silver Star about dark thirty. She invited Mack in, but he declined saying, "I should get back out to the Dead Dog and check on things. I've been gone a while. Besides, I am beat. How about I come get you for breakfast in the morning?"

"Sounds good." she said. She slid over and hugged him like she never wanted to let him go. She kissed him and got out of the truck. Mack walked her to the door, and again they hugged like they couldn't let go. They both knew now that their hearts would never let go. He broke the embrace and kissed her again and walked back to his truck. He waited, with his truck headlights on the front door, for her to get in the house.

As Sam put the key in the lock she noticed a business card stuck in the door. The card was from a lawyer in town. Written on the back was

Please call me concerning the estate of Buster Crabtree.

She sure didn't know what that was about. She put the card in her pocket and thought, *Maybe Buster left me a saddle or something. Isn't that sweet?*

CHAPTER 23

New Fortune

Mack arrived back at Sam's trailer the next morning, and he was feeling pretty good. He had a good night's sleep, without nightmares, in his own bed. The wheels were getting back on his wagon of life.

When she heard his truck pull up, Sam came out to meet him. She gave him a really big good morning kiss and hopped in the truck. As they drove back out to the main road Sam talked about lining out her day and getting her horses back on a schedule. She enjoyed the break but she was ready to get back to work. She asked, "What you got going today?"

"Today I'm going to dust off that saddle shop and get back to work. I got plenty of it waiting on me. I'm ready to make some saddles."

She smiled inside. She'd sensed that his spirit was calmer, and now she knew he really did leave his demons to drown at the coast. He was happier and calmer than she had seen him for a long time; this made her happier too.

They parked the truck at Jake and Dorothy's Café and went inside. The morning crew was still there with a few of the younger men starting to come in and settle. As they walked through the gauntlet of handshakes and howdies, the question on everyone's lips was, "Hey, Mack, how ya doin'? What about that fire chief?" All Mack could say was he didn't know anymore than they did. They were hungry for the inside scoop and were disappointed he couldn't feed it to them.

Mack and Sam made it to a table at the back and ordered some breakfast. While they were waiting on their food, Sam pulled the business card out of her pocket and handed it to Mack. She asked, "What do you make of this?"

He looked at it and said, "Hell if I know. I thought all that stuff was said and done. His office is just down the street, let's walk down there when we are done here."

Breakfast was finished and the last cup of coffee emptied. The two ran the gauntlet again with the second shift of the Jake and Dot's regulars asking, "Hey, Mack, what about that fire chief?"

"I don't know, I don't know."

They walked down the street to the law offices of Harvey Fleesum, attorney. They walked in the office and met the receptionist. Sam introduced herself, "Hello, I am Samantha—"

"I know who you are, Sam!" hollered the lawyer from his open office door. "Come on in here!"

They walked into Harvey's office. The walls were decorated with Remington and Russell paintings. Four big, mounted deer heads and various guns were also hung around the room. Harvey Fleesum was the quintessential west Texas lawyer.

They all shook hands and Harvey invited them to have a seat. He opened the meeting with, "Sam, I have been Buster's lawyer for a long time. The reason I wanted to meet with you is that you were mentioned in his will. I didn't invite you to the first reading of the will at his request. He figured he would save you from fighting with those rat bastard kids of his."

Sam was confused and said, "I don't get it. What is going on?"

Harvey laughed out loud and said, "Oh, you are going to get it, darlin'." He continued, "Buster called me to come meet with him at that place he was in up at Fort Worth. It was pitiful to see a man of that caliber in a hell hole such as that. Anyway, after his kids had gone up there and told him about his house burning down and then talked about putting him in a home so they could sell the place; well it pissed him off. He called me to change his will. I have it all recorded but I will just read you the transcript. Be advised these are all his words, just as he dictated them."

Sam looked at Mack who was just as confused as she was. The lawyer began to read:

> "Being of sound mind in a beat up body, I guess I'm supposed to say that, I am writing my new will. It ain't looking good for me, so I want to get some stuff lined out. To that pack of coyotes called my children, I leave whatever ya'll scavenged out of my burnt up house. You got it and I can't get it back, so it is yours. There you go.

As for my ranch and all that comes with it, I leave that to Samantha Nawaji. She is my friend and was always nice to this old man. I believe she is a great horsewoman and needs a good place.

I have three stipulations. She can't sell it to my no good brother, Bubba, even though I know she never would. I can trust her to keep it like I want it to be. She has to build a great training facility, and I know she can. She will build a bunkhouse for traveling rodeo cowboys to use at no charge when they are in town. My lawyer will inform her as to how this may be accomplished.

I want her and Mack to take my ashes up to that hill at the back of the property and spread them there. I always liked that spot. I have three horses left and she gets them, too. She has to keep them and care for them. When they finally die I want them buried up there on that hill with me. They are good horses — even that sonofabitch that broke my hip.

I reckon this is gonna start a shit-storm with my kids but that is too bad.

Ya'll were too busy to have anything to do with me for a long time, so ya'll just go back to being busy. It's all done and legal. It all belongs to Sam now."

The lawyer put the paper down and said, "I have to make a phone call now. If you will excuse me." He went to the outer office.

Sam was speechless. Tears were welling in her eyes. She looked at Mack, and he was slackjawed and could say nothing. Neither had the words. Sam had never been given anything in her life and she couldn't understand that all of the sudden she owned 500 acres of the best land in Erath county.

The lawyer returned to the room and sat down. He asked, "Well, what do you think?"

She found her voice and asked, "Is that it? I own Buster's place now?"

He laughed and said, "After you sign some papers, yes ma'am, you do. That and a little more. That part about me explaining how you were gonna do it? Well that part was left out so the kids wouldn't throw a bigger fit. They said they wanted to sue, but I explained to them it would go to an Erath county court with an Erath county judge who knew Buster and what he wanted. I helped them understand that they would be wasting money they did not have on a suit.

But anyway, what they don't know is that Buster had all the mineral rights to his land and Bubba's, too. When his parents drew up their will with my daddy a long time ago, they knew Buster would keep the land to be a ranch and not let the oil companies on it. Back then they tore everything up really bad when they drilled, not like today when they leave it nice and pretty. So, they gave all the minerals to Buster since they didn't trust Bubba to do the right thing.

Buster told me to tell you to go ahead and let the oil company on the land and that it will pay for all the work you need to do. I think it will most likely pay to have a top notch facility built, like he stipulated, and you will have quite a bit left over. They have been dogging him for years to lease the place but he wouldn't do it. I just placed a phone call to the top bidder for leasing the mineral rights and I expect he is setting the road on fire getting down here from Fort Worth as we speak."

Sam was still having a hard time wrapping her mind around what had just happened.

The lawyer said, "Let's get those papers signed and my secretary will run them to the courthouse so you will be the bona fide owner and can sign when that oil boy gets here. If that is what you want to do. If you should decide to sign with him, I would advise you to retain counsel and I would be happy to provide that service."

Sam had the "deer in the headlights" look when she turned to Mack for help. He smiled and nodded. So she said, "Uh, yeah. Okay."

Harvey had all the paperwork prepared and ready to sign. He explained pages and she signed. This went on for an hour. She signed the last one just as the oil company man came in the office. The oil company man explained to her what sort of work he expected to do on the ranch and the estimated earnings she would receive from the royalties. He was not high pressure and was very considerate. She felt good about him and agreed to do business with his company.

This led to more explaining and signing. She could tell that Harvey Fleesum was going to work well with her when he negotiated into the contract that the bull-dozers working on the drill site would also level out an area for stables and a covered arena. Sam hadn't even thought of that; things were moving so fast.

When the discussion of monetary compensation came up, it made her head swim. Quick rough cal-culations between her and Mack showed more than enough up-front money to start construction on a covered arena and boarding stables, and that included a nice apartment for her in the stables. The negotiations between Harvey and the oil man were a Ping-Pong game that Mack and Sam were just sitting by watching. Sam let it happen because she trusted Harvey, if Buster did then she could too, plus she didn't understand what was happening anyway.

The jumble of legalities took most of the day. Finally, the last paper was signed. The oil man stood up and stretched, he extended his hand and said, "Samantha, I am glad we came to terms on this. We both stand to make a lot of money on the deal. I look forward to working with you. We will begin work within the month. If you have any questions, call me any time." With that he was gone and headed back to Fort Worth.

Harvey laughed and said, "Man, what a day! Sam, when you got up this morning did you ever think you would be going to bed a rich woman?"

She was still in shock. She said, "Not in my wildest dreams did I ever think this would happen. It is a lot to take in. Thank you for all your help."

"You are sure welcome. I look forward to working with you. If I can be of any help just give me a call any time. I expect ya'll are going to want to go celebrate.

I think I will go home and take mama to dinner. Ya'll have a good night."

Sam and Mack stepped out of the office and walked back to his truck in front of the café. She asked Mack "What just happened today?"

He said, "I think you just had a dream come true."

She laughed and said, "Well let's continue the dream. Let's go get some steaks and cook them out at your place. My treat."

He said, "I like the way you think."

They went to the store and picked out the best steak in the rack and some vegetables to grill too. In the beer cooler she opted for the expensive beer, something she would never think to buy. After all, this was a celebration. When they pushed the buggy up to the checkout stand, Sam looked in her purse then at Mack and said, "Uh, can I borrow some money?"

CHAPTER 24

Back Home in Many Ways

Mack figured it could go either way. His return to the fire station family could be a welcoming event or the wheels could have come off the wagon and the place could be in turmoil. He knew the saving grace would be the old driver, Bear. As much as the crusty old fart enjoyed a good crisis or conspiracy, he also wanted a fire station to run like it should. He was very adept at using his verbal bullwhip to quell any dissidents.

This thought overshadowed the others spinning in his mind, since it would be the first to be dealt with.

How to help and guide Samantha with her fortunate turn of events could come later, if she even wanted his advice. He felt like they were getting emotionally closer but she was still very independent. Mack thought it best not to push his ideas on her uninvited.

Way in the back of his mind was the high impact event down on the coast. The whole time he was in his rage now seemed like a bad dream he was glad to wake up from. The magnitude of the event had driven out the demons that had plagued his mind and he was much happier now. Happy, too, that the event had no solid connection to him and, anyway, people in Port Mansfield did not talk to outsiders.

As he pulled into the station parking lot, he brought himself back to singular thought and said aloud, "Welcome back, Bud."

As was his habit for so many years, he went to the gear rack and grabbed his gear to put on the fire engine. On the hanger was a note that said: Welcome back, Lieutenant. He had been working up the macho bravado that would be necessary to re-enter the station environment. "Those weenies," he said to himself, but deep down he was touched.

After his gear was all properly situated on the fire engine, he went in the station day room where everyone was waiting. The regular morning shift change erupted in whoops and hollers, "Welcome back, Loo!" Back slaps and handshakes were the order of the morning. Mack swelled up his chest and hollered, "The sheriff is back in town! Now, get busy on a double throw down good breakfast! We got to fuel the machine, boys."

In amongst all this, Mack found the off-going Lieutenant, exchanged information and cut him loose. When the rest of the previous shift had all left, the crew fell into the duties of the day. Mack went to his office to see what he needed to catch up on. He felt relieved that all systems seemed normal. Morale seemed high and everyone seemed to still be on track. The officer who had taken his place had kept all the records up-to-date and the work was done.

In honor of the return of their Lieutenant, the rookies whipped up the requested big deal meal for breakfast. Omelets, fried potatoes, bacon, and biscuits and gravy were all on the table. Mack felt honored to be sitting at the table with all his brothers of the fire service. He had no orders of the day, he just wanted to get caught up on what all had happened since he had been gone.

While the crew ate the feast, Mack asked, "So, what did I miss while I was gone?"

Bear answered, "Well, I guess you already figured out we got a new interim Chief. Word on the street is he is going to get the job for good."

"Yeah, Chief Taylor is the one who put me back to work. I hope he gets the job. He would be a good one. So what happened there? What happened to Big Al?"

Bear was glad to have the floor to expound on his knowledge of the situation and his theories. "A few days after you got put off, Big Al was paid a visit. I heard a couple of Texas Rangers just walked right in his office and closed the door. The next day he was nowhere to be found. I don't know what happened, nobody downtown would say anything. Even my confidential sources had lockjaw. It had to be some big stuff going on to shut everybody up like that. I couldn't even get any info from my cop buddies. Everybody I talked to said they did not know a thing, like nobody in the city was informed of anything. Evidently, Big Al was gone-gone, because a few days after that we got the notice that Assistant Chief Taylor would be the new Interim Fire Chief."

Mack was glad his request for the use of the tape had been honored. He played along, "I wonder what could have happened to run him off like that?"

The rest of the crew had heard this from Bear many times before, and they were tired of it and kept eating. He continued, "Well, Junior came up missing before he could investigate that fire. They found his truck in a pasture outside of town. The cops, and I hear the Texas Rangers too, are looking for him. Think about it, Mack

— fatality fire, investigator missing under suspicious circumstances, Texas Rangers just walking in to Big Al's office unannounced, then Big Al skips town. Something sure smells fishy."

Mack chuckled inside at the unintended pun. "Dang, Bear, you are the know all of all know-it-alls and you can't find out anything? I'm losing faith in you, brother."

This insulted Bear just a little, he had always had pride in his investigative abilities. "Mack, nobody downtown or in this whole town for that matter, knows anything. I got nothing. I do know for a fact, though, that Big Al was rescued off an abandoned oil rig down in the Gulf of Mexico. There were two other guys with him. A friend of mine with the McAllen Fire Department called me to tell me that. He also told me the Rangers arrested the two other guys at the hospital. So, you tell me. Big Al was with two guys that were arrested. I don't think there is any question about him being dirty. I just can't tie it all together."

"Boy hid-ee, Bear, that's going to be some story when it all comes together. I'm sure you will keep up on it." Some of the men at the table snickered.

"You're damn straight I will. And you laughing sons-of-bitches won't be laughing then." Bear spread his stink eye all around the table then changed the subject.

"So, what did you do while you were off? Nobody saw you around town."

"Aw, since I had some time, I took a little road trip and ended up down on the coast to do some fishing."

"I figured you did something like that. Did you go by yourself?"

Mack took a drink of coffee and thought a minute. "I took another guy but I left him down there."

Bear had a strange smirk that Mack couldn't read. Bear said, "Well, while you were down there did you happen to see—"

Bear and breakfast were interrupted by the dispatch speaker giving alert tones and blaring "Engine 7. Engine 2. Engine 5. Truck 2. Respond to a structure fire 2500 Pioneer Drive. All units responding be advised caller states fire is coming through the roof." The firefighters stood in unison and headed to the door, with Mack bringing up the rear. He yelled to everybody, "Pull your boots up, boys, and let's go slay the dragon!"

Friends in High Places

Mack McWhirter travels to New Mexico to deliver saddles and see new country. He unwittingly discovers evil is real but so is Karma. His salvation is he has friends in high places.